Enrollment Form

☐ *Yes!* I WANT TO BE A *PRIVILEGED WOMAN*.
Enclosed is one *PAGES & PRIVILEGES™* Proof of
Purchase from any Harlequin or Silhouette book currently for
sale in stores (Proofs of Purchase are found on the back pages
of books) and the store cash register receipt. Please enroll me
in *PAGES & PRIVILEGES™*. Send my Welcome Kit and FREE
Gifts -- and activate my FREE benefits -- immediately.

More great gifts and benefits to come.

NAME (please print)
_____

ADDRESS   APT. NO
_____

CITY   STATE   ZIP/POSTAL CODE

**NO CLUB!
NO COMMITMENT!**
*Just one purchase brings
you great Free Gifts and
Benefits!*

Please allow 6-8 weeks for delivery. Quantities are limited. We reserve the right to
substitute items. Enroll before October 31, 1995 and receive one full year of benefits.

Name of store where this book was purchased_____
Date of purchase_____
Type of store:
    ☐ Bookstore   ☐ Supermarket   ☐ Drugstore
    ☐ Dept. or discount store (e.g. K-Mart or Walmart)
    ☐ Other (specify)_____

Which Harlequin or Silhouette series do you usually read?
_____

Complete and mail with one Proof of Purchase and store receipt to:
U.S.: *PAGES & PRIVILEGES™*, P.O. Box 1960, Danbury, CT 06813-1960
Canada: *PAGES & PRIVILEGES™*, 49-6A The Donway West, P.O. 813,
    North York, ON M3C 2E8

HT-PP5B

▼ DETACH HERE AND MAIL TODAY! ▼

Dear Reader,

Do *you* have a secret fantasy? Everybody does. Maybe it's to be rich and famous and beautiful. Or to start a no-strings affair with a sexy mysterious stranger. Or to have a sizzling second chance with a former sweetheart.... You'll find these dreams—and much more—in Temptation's exciting new yearlong promotion, Secret Fantasies.

The talented team of Shannon Harper and Madeline Porter, who write as Madeline Harper, contribute this month's story. Heroine Kasey Halliday has always longed to have a passionate, earth-shattering affair with a dark, enigmatic stranger. Her dreams come true when she meets her new neighbor, Will Eastman. But suddenly, mysterious "accidents" are starting to happen. And Kasey has to decide whether she can trust her fantasy lover...with her life.

In the coming months, look for Secret Fantasies books by Mallory Rush, JoAnn Ross and Glenda Sanders. Please write and let us know how you enjoy the "fantasy."

Happy Reading!

The Editors
c/o Harlequin Temptation
225 Duncan Mill Road
Don Mills, Ontario
M3B 3K9
Canada

Dear Reader,

Have you ever fantasized about being alone with a mysterious stranger? A man who's dark, handsome, charismatic and yet somehow...dangerous? We bet you have! His eyes meet yours, and the look that passes between you says a thousand words. Then he speaks and his voice is as compelling as the man himself. He fascinates you, and with his enigmatic power, he draws you closer.

Magically, your lives become entwined. It's as though Fate has ordained your meeting. He leads you down erotic paths and wraps you in a web of sensuality. But the feeling of danger lingers, and just as you surrender your heart, you discover he's not who he says he is. The ground shifts beneath your feet, and you begin to doubt your lover, now a stranger in your arms.

In this story, Will Eastman embodies all the charismatic charms of that stranger. He's a mysterious and devastatingly attractive hero, a man of deep emotions who's hiding a dark secret. Kasey Halliday is his match—a heroine of courage and conviction, who learns to trust her heart and the power of love.

As writers—and readers—of romantic suspense, nothing intrigues us more than a heady mix of love and danger, eroticism and mystery. We hope you find this combination as satisfying as we do.

So, settle back and enter Kasey's secret fantasy....

Sincerely,

Madeline Harper
a.k.a. Shannon Harper and Madeline Porter

"Lean forward," he ordered in a gentle voice, "and I'll massage your neck."

Obediently, Kasey dropped her head and felt Will's thumbs at the base of her neck. He moved them in a firm, circular motion that sent tremors racing along her nerve endings.

"I was right," he murmured. "Your muscles are in knots. But I can take care of that."

As he moved his hands over her body, Kasey's skin grew warm and pliant. She let out a deep sigh of contentment. The memory of her close call at the subway started to blur and then disappeared. She leaned back, amazed that she had ever been wary of him. His sense of authority, the coiled power beneath his smooth image and the whisper of arrogance in his voice were all things that had made him seem dangerous. Now those were the very same things that gave her a deep sense of security. She moaned.

He leaned close, his breath warm against her neck. "I'm crazy about the sound effects."

She flushed. "Sorry, I got carried away."

"Don't say you're sorry. You have no idea how much I want that to happen."

According to **Madeline Harper** "there's no place like New York." Both Shannon Harper and Madeline Porter, who write under the pseudonym of Madeline Harper, have lived in the Big Apple and visit every chance they get. So, when they were approached to write a story for Temptation's Secret Fantasies miniseries, what better setting could they find than the city that never sleeps, and "where anything can happen...and often does."

Books by Madeline Harper

HARLEQUIN TEMPTATION

326—THE JADE AFFAIR
389—THE WOLF
428—THE SUNDOWNER
447—WEDDING BELL BLUES
476—THE PIRATE'S WOMAN
499—CHRISTMAS IN JULY
527—THE TROUBLE WITH BABIES

Don't miss any of our special offers. Write to us at the following address for information on our newest releases.

Harlequin Reader Service
U.S.: 3010 Walden Ave., P.O. Box 1325, Buffalo, NY 14269
Canadian: P.O. Box 609, Fort Erie, Ont. L2A 5X3

STRANGER
IN MY ARMS
Madeline Harper

Harlequin Books

TORONTO • NEW YORK • LONDON
AMSTERDAM • PARIS • SYDNEY • HAMBURG
STOCKHOLM • ATHENS • TOKYO • MILAN
MADRID • WARSAW • BUDAPEST • AUCKLAND

To Marion Smith Collins,
who first opened the door to
Temptation

ISBN 0-373-25654-X

STRANGER IN MY ARMS

Copyright © 1995 by Madeline Porter & Shannon Harper.

1

"HOLD THE DOOR, please!" Kasey Halliday made a dash for the elevator as the doors began to close. She managed to get her foot in the crack just in time and pulled open a space big enough to slip through.

"Close call," she said breathlessly.

The only other passenger was a tall bearded man wearing dark glasses. He stared stolidly ahead as the elevator began its descent toward the Bartow Tower lobby, nineteen stories below.

An awkward silence surrounded them. Two strangers confined in a small enclosed space, keeping each other at a wary distance. Kasey glanced at her companion out of the corner of her eyes. She'd always been put off by people who wore dark glasses indoors. But on him, they seemed less an affectation than something more, well, mysterious, she decided.

Kasey was sure she'd never seen him in the building; she would have remembered. Tall and muscular, long-limbed and elegant, his dark brown hair fell a bit below his ears, fashionably long. His clothes were well cut and expensive: chocolate linen trousers and a rust-colored shirt that clung to his well-muscled shoulders and chest. Earth tones. Dark, sensual and very stylish, even in the summer. Of course, appearances could be deceiving, and a woman alone in New York City couldn't be too careful. At least, that's what she was always being told.

Ridiculous, Kasey thought. She rode the Bartow Tower elevators numerous times every day and never had the slightest problem with other passengers. 'Course, the elevators broke down fairly often, but the riders were always courteous. Anyway, the man wasn't paying any attention to her. He seemed lost in a private world all his own.

Then, as they passed the third floor, the elevator gave a shudder and a sickening grind before coming to a bumping halt. Kasey was flung across the car into the solid chest of the taciturn passenger.

"Sorry, I—" She attempted to disentangle her handbag, which was looped over his arm.

"What the hell's the matter?" The question was like a low accusatory growl.

"My handbag, I—"

"Not that. What happened to the elevator?" he asked as he grasped Kasey under the elbows and effortlessly lifted her away from him, pushing the handbag into her arms.

"We're stuck," she said. "Between the second and third floors."

Behind the sunglasses, his stare was dark, intimidating and focused on her. Kasey took two steps backward and pressed herself against the wall of the elevator. She could see the muscles in his neck tense, his jawline stiffen. What was going on with this guy? She watched warily as he turned from her and angrily jabbed at buttons on the elevator panel. The alarm began to sound, echoing eerily in the elevator shaft. He continued to push the buttons.

"That won't do any good," Kasey advised quietly. "The elevators are computerized, like everything else in this building."

"What do you suggest we do, just stand here and wait?"

Kasey bristled at his tone. "Eventually, the superintendent will throw some switches and we'll move again," she told him.

He turned to face her, pushing his glasses on top of his head.

Wow, she thought. Her first impression had been right. He was gorgeous in a dark, brooding way. High cheekbones, straight nose, broad forehead, presently creased in a frown. She couldn't tell much about his mouth under that beard, but his eyes were extraordinary, brown flecked with gold-and-green. The eyes of a jungle cat. A shiver ran along her spine. She tried to look away, but his gaze held her.

"How long will our rescue take?"

"I'm not sure," she admitted.

"What is it with this building?" There was an arrogance in his voice that told her he was a man used to getting answers. Fast. The air throbbed with his frustration.

Kasey gave an easy laugh, hoping to break the tension. "You mean you haven't heard about Bartow Tower, the Wonder of the West Side?" she asked, mimicking the newspaper ad.

"I thought this was a new luxury high rise." His voice was husky and low, with a dark, velvety undertone even when edged with impatience.

"It's all high-tech, but elevators still break down, power goes out and the automatic doors often lock tenants in the laundry room. Those of us who live here call it Bartow Horror. There are times when it seems as if the computer system has gone mad, and the building is deliberately trying to be hostile to the tenants. Sometimes, I—"

She broke off; he wasn't listening. He was studying the elevator car, his eyes tracing the limits of the small space, looking up at the ceiling as if it might present a way out. He was like a caged animal, a powerful panther trapped in a confined space. He exuded a dark, dangerous kind of energy, intimidating and fascinating.

Suddenly, he shook his head in disgust and leaned against the opposite wall. He was going to suffer and glower alone . . . and in silence.

The elevator car was so quiet, she could hear his deep, ragged breathing and the fast-paced beating of her own heart. There was something oddly intimate about the situation. Even a little romantic, she fantasized—a man and a woman trapped together in an elevator—except this man and woman weren't speaking.

She looked at her watch, frowned and then surreptitiously glanced at her companion. There was still an illusion of controlled energy emanating from him—and an undeniable sexuality.

The silence grew heavier and surrounded them like a thick blanket. Kasey looked up. He was studying *her*, she realized, his eyes narrowed and suspicious. She was reminded again of a jungle cat observing his prey.

She ran her fingers through her blond hair and straightened the lapel of her blazer. His gaze didn't waver, and it was unnerving. She wished she knew what he was thinking.

Ridiculous, Kasey decided. Two grown people, standing four feet apart and not saying a word. She broke the silence with the first thing that came into her head. "Are you new to the building?" God, what a stupid question, she thought, but it was too late.

"Subletting," he replied.

Again, silence. Common sense told her to keep her mouth shut. This guy had a wall around him eight feet tall. But Kasey never listened to advice, not even her own.

"I live in 1903," she volunteered. "Great view."

"I'm in 1905."

Next door! Kasey was encouraged to go on. "I knew Jim O'Hara was going on a long holiday, three months in Spain and France." She was thoughtful for a moment. "I didn't know he was renting the apartment out. Are you a friend of Jim's?"

He looked at her coolly, as if to say that it was none of her business. Which it wasn't, Kasey had to admit, but she hadn't been able to resist asking.

"I got the place through a rental agent," he said finally. Body rigid, eyes wary, he seemed on guard.

Again she noted the low, husky voice. It went with the image of a tall, dark, handsome—and unapproachable—stranger.

"Jim's trip is going to be great, backpacking through the Pyrenees. I'd love to travel. I—" Kasey stopped herself in midsentence. She talked too much, and she knew it. Asked too many questions, started conversations with strangers. Even after two years in New York City, she hadn't lost her smalltown openness. It took willpower, which she tried to exert now, closing her mouth firmly. The next conversational gambit was up to him.

Muffled voices interrupted the silence echoing up the elevator shaft.

"Sounds as though help is on the way," he said. "It took them long enough." Impatience vibrated in his voice.

"Mr. Lemnos, the superintendent, is down in the basement checking the cables. Pretty soon, we'll be moving again."

"You seem to know the routine. How long have you lived here?"

"About a year." Kasey was encouraged by his question, which gave her the opportunity to get an introduction going. "I'm Kasey Halliday. Your next-door neighbor."

To her surprise, a half smile played around his lips. Gone—at least for the moment—was the suspicion.

"I'm Will Eastman."

"Nice to meet you." Silence again. She checked her watch once more and spoke a little defensively. "I'm anxious to get out of here, too. I don't want to be late for work. I've just gotten a promotion, and I'd hate to start out this way."

"Do you work nearby?"

"Not too far. I work in a restaurant down near Columbus Circle. Walk-by-Windows. I'm the assistant manager."

"I've seen the place," he admitted.

"You should come by for dinner sometime. We have a great French chef. But he makes other dishes, too, not just French cuisine. Everything we serve is good. No, not just good, *formidable,* as the French would say." Kasey knew she was babbling.

Amusement glittered in his eyes. "Your enthusiasm is contagious, Ms. Halliday."

Again, his eyes held hers. She had the strangest compulsion to move toward him. Nervously, she wet her lips and swallowed hard. He looked at her with a gaze that was now interested, appraising.

Then, with an unexpected lurch, the elevator started, hurtling rapidly downward.

"Hold on," Will warned. "Who knows if the damned thing will stop."

Kasey grasped the shiny brass handrail as the elevator stopped smoothly and slowly, as if it had never been interrupted in its journey. The door slid open. Will Eastman didn't move.

"The lobby," Kasey said unnecessarily. The gleaming black-and-white marble floor stretched before them.

She saw the sudden surprising and charming quirk of his lips again. "I know, but I'm going to the basement," he told her.

She looked at him questioningly and was surprised when he decided to explain. "Have to see Mr. Lemnos about repairs on O'Hara's apartment." He touched the Open button and held the door for her.

"Thanks. It was nice to have company." Kasey stepped through the door. It shut before she heard his answer. If there was one. Well, she thought, so much for the interlude with her mysterious neighbor.

"Hey, there, Ms. Halliday." The doorman waved at her. "So you were trapped on number two."

"Again." Kasey stopped by the doorman's desk where Tim balanced on his stool. Round, rotund and nosy, he was noted for his obsessive interest in the tenants' lives. "The second time this month." She thought for a moment and then plunged ahead. "There was a guy on the elevator with me. Eastman, 1905."

There was nothing wrong with trying to find out about him, she told herself. After all, they were neighbors.

Tim made an officious show of checking his tenant list. "Yep, that's his name. Sublet 1905, but I didn't see him move in." He scratched his chin. "Must have done it at night." He made that sound ominous. "Well, we got so many people coming and going now, who can keep up?" Tim sighed eloquently. "Keeps me on my toes. Still a lot of vacancies. Two on your floor—1901 and 1906."

"Maybe people are catching on that Bartow Tower can be hazardous to their health. I ought to report the latest breakdown to the tenants' committee but I'm late, as it is. Would you get me a taxi, Tim?"

"Right-o. Anything for my favorite tenant."

And for a tip, Kasey thought, pulling a bill from her wallet. But why not? She had just received a promotion and a raise. The assistant manager of Walk-by-Windows could afford to take a cab now and then. She even had a good excuse for being late. An adventure, kind of, with Will Eastman—tall, dark, handsome and becoming more fascinating by the moment.

WILL EASTMAN temporarily disappeared from Kasey's mind as she became swept up in the whirlwind of work. At its core was Carl Dandridge, who tracked her down in the cubbyhole that she used as an office.

"Enjoying yourself, Kasey?" He stood at the door, arms folded belligerently across his narrow chest, his fists positioned in an attempt to create biceps. Hostility glittered in his pale blue eyes.

Kasey stood up, her eyes level with Carl's. "I'm working, Carl, and I understand from Fred Tomlinson that you already picked up your severance check."

"Yeah, I got my check, but I'm not finished here."

She heard the veiled threat but decided not to be intimidated by it. "All right, Carl. What do you want?"

"My job back."

"That's not within my power, and even if it were—"

"Yeah, you got me fired so why would you want me back?" he asked with a sneer.

"I never—"

"You lied about me to Tomlinson."

"Carl, that's not true. I never said a word to Fred about you—even though I was onto your game. When he offered me the job of assistant manager, it was because I earned it."

"I was framed," he yelled, "and you know it. You and that Judy Fiore bitch conspired against me. You got my job, and she got yours."

He took a step forward. Kasey could smell the liquor on his breath, but she held her ground and kept her voice steady. Yet she was trembling inside. Why? He was small and skinny—but wiry. His threats—and the hatred in his eyes—were real. And her office was at the end of a narrow hall that led to the pantry. Even if she screamed, no one would hear her.

"When Fred comes back, you can take this up with him. I can't do anything about it."

"You took my job, you blond bitch."

"No, I—"

He made a low guttural sound deep in his throat. "That Tomlinson bastard, firing me and then leaving town, afraid to face me."

Kasey kept her voice firm. "He's on vacation, Carl."

"He'll be running if he knows what's good for him, and you better run, too."

"I'm not afraid of you, Carl." Kasey reached for the phone. "And if you don't leave right now, I'll call the police."

His lips curled in an ugly grimace, and his eyes challenged hers.

Kasey lifted the receiver, praying her fingers were steady enough to dial 911. Her eyes remained locked with Carl's. She was determined not to look away. But she had to look down at the phone to punch in the numbers.

That's when Carl reached out to stop her. Still holding on to the phone, she drew back, her bravado replaced by heart-pounding fear.

Suddenly, an unexpected clink of crystal on crystal filled the silence and a busboy appeared from the pantry, pushing a cart of champagne glasses. Kasey let go of the frightened breath she'd been holding.

The boy stopped at the door, gave Carl a hard look and then glanced at Kasey. "Everything all right?"

"Yes, Bobby. Carl's leaving now."

Carl's eyes never lost their hard edge. "This isn't over, Kasey. I want my job back and I'll get it even if I have to go over Tomlinson's head. So stay out of my way. I'm warning you." He pushed past the busboy and stomped down the hall.

His mouth hanging open, Bobby watched Carl's retreating back and then looked at Kasey. "I—I had to go to the pantry to get extra glasses," he stammered. "For that special party."

"Oh, yes, the engagement party." She paused and took a deep breath, as if to calm her racing heart. "Was I glad to see you! Thanks," she added with genuine feeling. Her knees were still shaking. She hated confrontation of any kind. And the run-in with Carl was particularly upsetting.

She closed the door, wishing she could lock it. For a moment, she thought about escaping to the warmth of the kitchen or finding Judy in the dining room, but she decided against it. After all, the busboy knew she was here, and that fact alone would keep Carl away, she hoped. Anyway, one look at her desk told her that she wasn't going anywhere.

The desk was a disaster. An explosion of telephone messages covered its surface, as well as patron comments and complaints, time sheets and staff schedules—all the details that the manager, Fred Tomlinson, had left behind for her to handle. Walk-by-Windows opened for dinner at five-thirty, and there was a lot to do before she could leave the office.

She glanced at the door, still not comfortable with the idea that Carl might be lurking around somewhere. She dragged a chair over and secured it underneath the doorknob then gave the knob a pull. The door remained firmly shut, and she sat down to work.

BY FIVE-FIFTEEN, Walk-by-Windows was ready for business. Kasey did her final survey of the dining room with its floor-to-ceiling windows that looked out on a bustling New York street scene. Green and white awnings fluttered in the faint afternoon breeze, and Kasey nodded with satisfaction. All ready—with fifteen minutes to go.

Everything seemed cool and serene. Despite the frantic activity behind the scenes, Walk-by-Windows ran like clockwork. And in her new position, that's exactly the way Kasey wanted it to remain. So far today, she'd handled the usual problems, plus one—Carl Dandridge.

Judy Fiore waved to her from the bar. "Do we have time?"

"Yep," Kasey called out as she headed toward her friend. "The first reservation isn't until six. The big rush begins at eight with the engagement party, and then it's nonstop. Let's have our ice tea." She nodded to the bartender.

Mack, who ran his domain with an iron hand, poured the tea into tall, ice-filled glasses, topped them with slices of lemon and sent the two women toward their special corner table. There, checking to see that no one was watching, they indulged in their nightly ritual, glass clinking against glass.

"Here's to Kasey Halliday, the best damned assistant manager—currently acting as manager—of the best damned restaurant in New York. Is that superlative or not?"

"Possibly a little exaggerated, but I'll drink to it," Kasey said, clinking her glass again. "and to Judith Ann Fiore, the best service staff supervisor in the entire United States. No, the whole Western Hemisphere."

"No exaggeration there," Judy said as she took a big gulp of tea. "And it's certainly true today. Every service person present and accounted for, every table assigned." She leaned forward. "Now for the problem. I saw Carl slinking out the door but I never saw him slinking *in*, which bothers me. When did he get in, how did he get in and what did he want?"

"I don't know the answer to the first two questions, unfortunately. But I'm going to review security, believe me. As for what he wanted—his job back."

"That'll be the day."

"He thinks you and I conspired to get him fired."

Judy let out a snort and then looked around quickly. "Sorry! Sometimes I forget I work in such a classy place. But give me a break! Everyone but Fred Tomlinson knew Carl was taking kickbacks from half our suppliers."

"And padding the accounts of the others."

"And harassing the female staff, including me. It's a miracle he lasted as long as he did. Fred *was* pretty dim about the situation. She paused and gave Kasey a meaningful look. "No, not dim, just preoccupied with schmoozing with customers."

Kasey laughed. "But he finally caught on. And Carl's not too happy about it."

Her dark eyes bright with concern, Judy studied Kasey's face. "You're worried about Carl, aren't you?"

"Maybe. A little," she confessed.

"Well, you should be. He's a sneaky devil. I'd watch my back."

"I will, but Carl's a bully, pure and simple. I doubt if he'll show up here again, especially since I threatened to call the police. He knows I would have done it. We've seen the last of him."

"Don't be too sure," Judy said.

"Carl's all talk and no action, Judy. Trust me. I know the man."

Judy rolled her eyes. "Pu-leez, Kasey, I'm your buddy, remember?"

The two women grinned at each other. They'd been friends since the day they both started as waitresses two years ago at Walk-by-Windows. As other employees came and went, they stayed on and earned their promotions.

"And as your buddy," Judy continued, "I know you're not a great judge of male character."

"Don't start with me," Kasey warned.

Judy ignored her. "Let's see. There was Jean-Paul, the former sous-chef, incredibly handsome, I'll admit . . ."

"I thought he wanted to be friends and improve his English," Kasey said. "How was I supposed to know he wanted to marry me for a green card?"

"The guy you met cycling . . ."

"Great legs," Kasey said, finishing her ice tea. "But unfortunately, terminally unemployed."

"And Mr. Wonderful, the actor you followed to New York."

"Back in Springfield now, happily selling appliances. Things worked out for the best. And none of those relationships was serious, Judy. I learned from them, and they certainly didn't turn me off to men."

Judy regarded her friend thoughtfully for a moment. "You know your problem, Kasey?"

Kasey groaned. "If I don't, I'm sure you'll tell me."

"You're too damned friendly."

"And I intend to stay that way. I won't live my life being afraid to reach out to people. That's not me."

"Friendly is okay—within reason—but sometimes you push friendliness into impulsiveness."

"I use good judgment. Usually." Kasey grinned at her friend. "Sometimes."

Judy frowned and pursed her lips. "You have to remember, Dorothy, you're not in Kansas anymore."

"I'm not Dorothy, and this certainly isn't Oz. Besides, I'm from Missouri, not Kansas," Kasey reminded her.

"Whatever. To a native New Yorker, anything west of the Hudson River is confusing," Judy said airily. "You're too trusting, and sometimes—"

Laughter danced in Kasey's eyes as she interrupted. "Then I guess you don't want to hear about the man I met in the elevator."

"At Bartow Horror?"

"Where else?"

"Tell me every word. And it better be good."

BEFORE RELATING the elevator saga, Kasey checked out the restaurant one more time with Judy in tow. "Do you think the color scheme is too much?" she asked her friend.

"Dark green tablecloths with a touch of pink in the candles and flowers? That's a change you talked Fred into, Kasey. What's your problem?"

"I don't know. It's clean, uncluttered, sophisticated. But it's also very trendy. Maybe too much so."

"Trends are good. Shows you're on top of things. Now, about the guy in the elevator?"

"I'm going for paper white narcissus next week, instead of pink baby carnations," Kasey decided.

"Fine. It'll be another nice change. Now, about the guy. You brought him up, Kasey. So forget the flowers and tell all."

"Flowers are real."

"And the guy isn't?"

"I don't know," Kasey said. "Maybe he's a fantasy."

"You dreamed him up?" Judy asked as she led Kasey back to their table.

"No, he was there—on the elevator—and he was..." She searched for the right word. "Gorgeous," she finally proclaimed.

"So what's the problem?" Judy asked.

"He was also sort of . . ."

"What, Kasey?"

"Mysterious. Brooding. Sexy. Maybe even a little dangerous-looking." She shot Judy an anticipatory look.

"Oh, great," Judy groaned. "Just the kind of guy you need in New York City. What do you mean 'dangerous'?"

"Well, he was wearing dark glasses in the elevator—"

"Uh-oh," Judy interrupted. "On the run from the law. Yeah, I can see how he'd be dangerous."

"He wasn't like that. He was more—aloof. He had a real attitude about him. I kept thinking of—" She broke off.

"You're making me crazy. Tell, tell. What were you thinking?"

Kasey's voice took on a dreamy edge. "Hmm, well, he reminded me of a big jungle cat. Like a panther. Caged against his will. And he had the greatest eyes, golden, kind of."

Judy put her hand on Kasey's forehead. "Yep, you're feverish."

Kasey laughed. "Okay, I'm fantasizing like crazy, but he was drop-dead gorgeous and had a great body. Tall and lean but well-built. When he picked me up—"

"Picked you up?"

"When the elevator stopped, I kind of fell into him, and he disentangled me."

"Hmm," Judy said thoughtfully. "This could have possibilities. What does he do?"

"I don't know," Kasey admitted.

"Where's he from?"

"Don't know."

"Well, what *do* you know about him?"

Kasey was beginning to feel defensive. "I know his name. Will Eastman. I know where he lives. On my floor, next door to me, in fact. He's subletting."

Judy sighed deeply. "A mysterious stranger who's moved in next door. This is beginning to sound less like a fantasy and more like a mistake, Kasey."

"No, I—"

"Kasey, did you tell him about yourself, where you work, that you live alone—"

"No. Not exactly," Kasey defended. "I might have mentioned Walk-by-Windows, but I was very circumspect. Despite what you think, I don't go around giving out my life history to strangers." Then her voice lost its defensiveness, and she grinned impishly. "Even to romantic strangers with great-looking clothes and expensive haircuts."

"Promise me one thing," Judy demanded. "Before you go out with him, learn the facts. A woman can't—"

"Be too careful," Kasey finished for her. "Yeah, I know. But don't worry. I'm not going out with him. In fact, I'll probably never get a chance to talk with him again—unless we get stuck in the elevator."

Judy laughed. "At Bartow Horror, there's always a chance of that."

"He was just a little afternoon adventure," Kasey said thoughtfully. "Something to liven up the day."

"And that something lives next door to you, so be careful."

Kasey pushed back her chair and stood up. "Judy Fiore, you're the most suspicious person I've ever met."

"I'm from New York. It goes with the territory."

"First, you try to frighten me with warnings about Carl sneaking up on me, and now you tell me to watch out for a guy I've only seen once. Carl's not going to be a problem. And my adventure with Will Eastman is over, done . . . forgotten."

"Except in your overactive imagination."

"A little fantasy never hurt anyone," Kasey protested.

"As long as it stays a fantasy."

"I know the difference," Kasey said adamantly. "I really do."

WILL COULDN'T GET the woman on the elevator out of his head. He'd been tempted to ask the building superintendent about her, or maybe talk to the doorman— the nosy one, Tim, who thought he knew everything.

But it wouldn't be a smart move to make himself conspicuous by asking questions about another tenant. It could be foolish. And maybe dangerous.

Will knew he should put her out of his mind. Problem was, he couldn't. And thinking about her made him restless and edgy, eager to escape his high-rise prison. He glanced through the balcony doors at the twilight sky. There was still an hour until nightfall. He settled down to wait.

2

THE DAY WAS HOT and muggy. It wasn't the best time to be wrestling with a box of winter clothes, Kasey realized. But the tiny closet in her bedroom was filled to capacity, and it was time to move out the stuff she hadn't worn in a couple of years. That meant storage. In the Bartow Tower subbasement.

She pushed the big box of clothes into the hall and almost ran over her neighbor, Glenna Ivy.

"Whoops." Glenna dodged the box. "Just the person I want to see. I need a favor."

Kasey laughed. "After almost running you down, I guess I owe you one. So, yes, I'll feed Lo Mein this weekend."

"How did you know?"

"I'm psychic." Kasey put her fingers to her forehead, closed her eyes and pretended to go into a trance. "You're wearing shorts, a T-shirt and baseball cap," she intoned dramatically. "You have a duffel bag over your shoulder, it's Friday—and you own a share in a house at the shore." Kasey opened her eyes. "However, Lo doesn't like sand, much less saltwater."

"Is it too much trouble? I can ask Tim—"

"Please, keep Tim out of this. He's nosy enough, as it is. And it's no trouble for me to feed the cat. I still have your extra key from last time."

"A million thanks, Kasey. His food is on the kitchen counter, and his litter is in the bathroom."

"I know the routine. And Lo Mein and I are friends—kind of."

"I'll be back on Sunday," the tall, leggy brunette promised.

"Have fun."

Glenna was on the way to the elevator, when Kasey beckoned to her. Curiosity, as usual, had gotten the best of Kasey, and she wanted Glenna's input. Since they were close in age, the two women often shared stories of their love lives—or lack of them. Glenna possessed a wry sense of humor about her experiences in the "dating wars," as she called her social life.

Kasey lowered her voice. "Have you seen the new guy in 1905?"

"Nope, haven't seen a soul. Did Jim rent out his place?"

"It's a sublet deal through an agent. Name's Will Eastman."

"Attractive?" Glenna, too, spoke in a near whisper. "More important, eligible?"

"Yes to attractive, and as for eligible..." She shrugged. "He's living there alone, I think. But he's also very mysterious. I've only seen him once—in the elevator. Tim says he moved in at night."

Glenna's brown eyes danced. "Maybe he can't take the sun." She seemed to warm up to that thought. "Or maybe he's a vampire!"

Kasey laughed. "Or he could just want his privacy. He's certainly not what you'd call friendly."

"But in the looks department, a number—"

"Ten, definitely."

"Well, if anyone can find out about him, you can. You're the nineteenth floor's unofficial housemother. Keep me posted. Hey, there's the elevator. Got to run! Thanks again."

Kasey stacked a few more items on top of the box, including an old quilt that had belonged to her grandmother, and a pair of ski boots. As she double-locked her apartment door, she thought about Glenna's remark. Was she really the floor's housemother? And if so, should she take that as a compliment? It *was* second nature for her to be outgoing and generous, offering to help with pet- and plant-sitting, picking up mail or running occasional errands when a neighbor was ill.

In the small town where she grew up, Kasey knew almost everyone in her neighborhood. Maybe she was foolish to try to re-create that same feeling on the nineteenth floor of a Manhattan apartment building. But she couldn't help it; friendliness was part of Kasey's personality, whether Manhattan liked it or not.

After pushing her load across the hall, she hit the button for elevator number one, which hadn't broken down in at least a month. It was the odds-on favorite to get her safely down to Bartow Tower's storage room.

THE BUILDING WAS less than two years old, but the subbasement might have belonged to another era. Probably because there wasn't a glimmer of natural light, only the dim illumination given off by bulbs suspended from the ceiling, casting eerie flickering shadows on the gray concrete walls.

"Trust the management," Kasey muttered to herself, "to save on the electric bill with forty-watt bulbs." The storage area was at the end of a narrow hall that was confining and dismal. It made her think of the dank passage deep inside a pyramid, where, of course, she'd never been, but she'd read enough mysteries to make the connection.

Heavy steel-plated gates enclosed the area. Kasey punched the computer code into a console, swung the gate open, shoved her box inside but didn't close the gate all the way. It was supposed to open automatically from the inside, but she had learned not to trust anything computerized at Bartow Tower.

Pushing the box ahead of her, Kasey made her way to the space assigned to the nineteenth floor and turned the key in the lock for cubicle 1903. Before opening the door, she looked around the storage area, searching the shadows that hugged every corner.

Kasey shivered. She was jumpier than usual, and she knew why. During a crazy couple of days, she'd been threatened by a disgruntled employee, confounded by a stranger in an elevator and warned about both men—and her own naïveté—by her closest friend. These incidents, combined with the gloom and isolation of the basement, were getting to her, generating uncomfortable questions. Could Carl have tracked her home to Bartow Tower? Could the stranger on the elevator somehow be a threat? She'd certainly told him enough to make herself vulnerable.

"You're fantasizing again, Kasey," she lectured herself. "Get the damned junk stored and get out of here." She pushed past her bike, promising herself to bring it

out again when the weather cooled, moved a pile of
books and began to put her belongings on a shelf.

But she was still spooked. She took a deep breath,
hearing Judy's warning reverberating in her mind. *A
woman can't be too careful.* Well, she'd left the heavy
gate to the hall open in case she needed to get out of the
area in a hurry. There was nothing more she could do.
And she was damned if she would get paranoid about
a disgruntled employee who had bullied her and a
mysterious man who had moved into her building. She
hung the boots by their laces on a hook and put up the
plastic-wrapped quilt.

Then she heard it.

A noise. It wasn't her imagination. And it wasn't one
of the everyday noises she normally heard in the building. Footsteps. They didn't sound brisk and forthright
but soft and furtive. And they were creeping toward
her. Kasey fought a moment of blind panic—and lost.
She pulled the door of her unit shut, pressed her back
against the side and tried to disappear in the darkness.

What if it *was* Carl? Maybe she'd been wrong about
his being nothing but a bully. Maybe her threat to call
the police had enraged him even more. What if he'd got
past the doorman, an easy-enough feat if Tim had been
gossiping with a tenant or flagging down a cab. What
if Carl had followed her into the basement—

Kasey's heart was beating fiercely, and she could hear
the rush of blood in her ears as the steps kept coming
closer and closer. Then they stopped, right in front of
her door. She held her breath and listened to the sound
of keys rattling. Whoever it was, he'd never get in here;

she had the only key. Her fingers closed tightly around it, and she tried not to make a sound. She could hear breathing, not hers, but the other person's. The person who was standing outside, waiting, listening.

After a long moment, the footsteps moved on, but not far, just to the unit next to hers. That was enough for Kasey. It gave her time to think, and act. Slowly, quietly, she inched open her door, exposing a narrow slit of light. Then she saw him, his back silhouetted against the light. It wasn't Carl but a tall man, big and muscular. He had a weapon in his hand, a long, dark instrument of death.

Kasey did the only thing possible—pushed open the door, surged out of her storage cubicle and ran like hell for the gate.

"What the—"

Kasey heard his astonished voice and then a thud behind her as the door hit him. She didn't stop running until she reached the steel gate and burst through, slamming it behind her. She was safe, for the moment, but he was on her heels. Never mind. The gate would stop him. She raced for the elevator and hit the button. She could hear it descending. He must have reached the gate by now. Kasey dared to cast a quick look over her shoulder.

Then darkness descended on her.

The bare bulb over her head blinked and went out. The elevator whirred to a stop somewhere high above her. Kasey's knees went weak, and she leaned back against the wall. Fear coursed through her, the deep primeval, instinctual fear of the dark. Blackness wrapped around her like a thick blanket, engulfing her, smothering her.

The intense silence was broken only by the rasping sound of her breath. Where was her pursuer? What was he doing?

It wasn't Carl; she knew that now. But someone else had followed her into the basement, and when she got away, he'd somehow caused the electrical system to shut down! But how? Why?

Kasey's mind was racing furiously. There wasn't time to worry about what had happened. Darkness surrounded her, but it surrounded him, too! This was her chance to escape.

She groped along the wall, searching for the stairwell door. If she could make it to the stairs ahead of him, she had a chance.

Her hand found the knob, and she turned it frantically. The door didn't budge. She pounded on it, hoping for help, and was suddenly flooded in light.

She turned around and looked toward the light, her eyes blinded. Whoever was after her had a flashlight. She covered her eyes.

"Turn it off, please! I'm not going anywhere."

The light moved away, and as she stood frozen, it danced erratically around the basement, searching the corners of the hall. Then it went out.

She wanted to scream, but her throat had constricted. The flashlight flicked back on. Whoever was holding it wasn't moving toward her. He wasn't moving at all. She suddenly realized that when the lights had shut down, so had everything else electrical. He was trapped behind the steel gate!

She breathed a sigh of relief and managed to call out, "Who are you? Why are you chasing me?"

The voice that answered was low and husky. "I could ask you the same question." She knew that voice. It was the man from the elevator, Will Eastman, and the weapon in his hand wasn't a gun but a flashlight! She felt like an idiot.

"But I know who you are," he said. "The woman in the elevator."

"Y-yes," she stammered. "Kasey. Kasey Halliday."

"But I don't know why you locked me in the storage room."

"Because, because . . . you chased me," Kasey told him. She still hadn't moved from her place against the wall.

"No . . . Kasey," he said. "You tore through the door and almost knocked me down." Then he apparently noticed her very clear body language and added, "You're really scared, aren't you?"

"Of course I am, with you skulking around—"

"Skulking? Me?"

"What are you doing in the subbasement, anyway?" she challenged.

"The same thing you are, I imagine. Putting some things in storage. This *is* the storage area, right?"

"Yes," she admitted.

"And I'm locked in. Because *you* closed the gate."

"I was afraid. I didn't know who you were, or what you were doing down here. All right," she admitted, "maybe I overreacted a little." She felt embarrassed but still defensive. "I had no idea the power would go off. You can't blame me for that, too."

"What do you mean, 'too'?"

"You acted as though it was my fault we were trapped on the elevator, and now you're blaming me again."

"I'm not blaming you and, by the way, I'm the one who's trapped," came the sardonic response.

Kasey bristled. "I'm not staying here by choice. The elevator's gone out . . ."

"What about the stairwell?"

"I tried it. The door's locked."

"Well, if I could get out of here . . ."

"What would you do that I can't?" she asked.

"I don't know. Something. Hell, I could be in here for hours."

"That's possible," Kasey agreed. "We both could. Since everything seems to be knocked out, it could be more than just this building . . ."

"What do you mean?"

"The weather has been unusually hot, everyone's running air conditioners . . ."

"You mean, a total power failure?"

"It happened last summer. I remember . . ." Kasey caught herself. Given their situation, she was sure, he wasn't interested in her stories about the last power outage.

"A total power failure," he repeated. "Great. Just great."

"I don't like it any better than you do," she said in frustration.

"But you're out there. And I'm in here."

For a moment, Kasey thought about that. She was both glad and sorry. If he were outside the gate, maybe he could help her find a way to escape; on the other hand, she felt somehow relieved that the gate separated them. Why, she didn't know. Fear, maybe. Or . . . what? She shook off the unexplainable feeling.

"Could you come over here, at least, so I don't have to shout?" he asked.

"I . . . I can't see . . ."

He shone the flashlight at her feet and then moved it backward, slowly, as she left her place by the wall and walked closer to the gate.

"Kasey Halliday," he said as she got close to him.

"Yes?"

He chuckled softly. It was a low seductive sound that sent a little prickle of anticipation along her spine.

"What's so funny?"

"Us." He laughed again. "We've got to stop meeting like this. People will talk."

Kasey responded to his teasing voice and laughed too. She could feel the tension begin to drain from her. "Sorry I snapped at you. I usually don't behave that way. None of this is your fault—or mine." She was standing a few feet from him, separated by the locked gate.

"Ironic, isn't it?" he asked her. "We've been imprisoned twice by Bartow Tower. Fate seems to be throwing us together."

"I'd call it spooky, but that's the wonderful charm of Bartow. The unexpected," Kasey said sarcastically.

"I'm catching on to the place. You're right—it's a horror show of sorts."

Tired of standing, Kasey sank next to the gate and leaned back, her arms wrapped around her knees.

Will sat down by her on the other side of the gate. He turned off the flashlight, and they were enveloped by impenetrable darkness. But she could sense his nearness. She could hear his slow, even breathing and the shifting of his body as he made himself comfortable. There was the same sensation of ambiguous intimacy that she'd felt on the elevator with him, an undercurrent of excitement that she couldn't deny. Will's voice came softly through the darkness. "I've even had a mysterious intruder."

"Someone broke into your apartment?" Kasey was truly startled. Despite its many problems, Bartow had been almost crime-free.

"Not someone. Something. A damned cat. Sort of beige color—"

Kasey laughed. "It's only Lo Mein. He belongs to a neighbor, and one of his favorite tricks is to jump from balcony to balcony. He also likes to visit. If you leave your doors open, he'll go right into your living room."

"So I've noticed," Will replied dryly.

"You won't be bothered this weekend," Kasey reassured him. "Glenna, the cat's owner, has gone to the shore, and I'm keeping Lo locked up. In fact, you and I and the cat are probably the only tenants on the floor this weekend. A couple of apartments are vacant, and the Kramers always go to—"

She broke off. Smart, Kasey, she chided herself. Very smart. Announcing that you and Will are alone on the nineteenth floor. Judy would have a fit if she heard you'd told him all that.

"The Kramers, you were saying..." His face was close to hers, separated only by the wire gate.

She shuffled a little and moved a few inches away.

"Sometimes," she lied, "the Kramers go to their cabin upstate." In fact, they went every weekend in the summer, but she wasn't going to tell him that.

"I've noticed that the city clears out on weekends."

"Especially in the summer." Now it was her chance, she realized, to find out more about Will. "How about you? Do you usually stay in town on the weekends?"

"Sometimes."

Well, that question had got her nowhere, she thought.

He shifted again, and she saw the illuminated dial of his watch glow in the darkness. "How long did the last one of these power outages last?" he asked.

"Um . . . about . . . three hours."

He groaned.

"But it may not be a citywide outage. Or even a West Side one. It could be only Bartow Tower."

"Even worse," he reminded her.

She laughed. "True. But even the elevator was only out for a few minutes. Most of the computer problems here don't last very long."

"Maybe not. But they make up for that in their frequency. I've lived here for five days, and I've already been stranded twice. Maybe it's time to take the owner to task—if not to court," he suggested.

"That in itself is a problem. He lives out of the country, in the Bahamas. So he's virtually unreachable."

"What about the management company?"

"They make a lot of promises but do little. We have a pretty strong tenants' association, though, and we try to keep the pressure on. Maybe you'd like to join?"

He chuckled again. "Nope. I don't think so. I'm not much of a joiner."

Kasey wasn't surprised to hear that admission from a man who came across as the quintessential loner. Still, she was determined to learn more about him. And maybe this was the perfect place. They were close, almost touching. But the gate kept her safe from him and from herself, from the mixed feelings that coursed through her, a tantalizing blend of safety and danger.

She struggled to clear her head and come up with an interesting question. But before she could pose it, the lights flickered on, then off, and finally on again.

Will was up in a flash, pushing at the gate. It didn't budge. "Quick, input the code before everything goes down again."

Kasey rushed to the console and started to hit the numbers. Then, for a split second, she hesitated.

"Kasey—" The lights were flickering again.

Trying to ignore her suspicions, Kasey tapped in the code and heard the click as Will opened the gate.

Then the flickering lights went out. Kasey couldn't see Will in the dark, but she could hear him moving toward her. Oh, Lord, what had she done? She froze, waiting.

3

WHEN WILL REACHED for Kasey, she quickly moved away, and he withdrew his hand. This wasn't the time to make her more nervous. Instead, he waited quietly beside her until the lights went back on. Then he said, softly but firmly, "Let's get to the elevator while there's still power."

"The storage room . . . I haven't finished—"

"Neither have I. Do you want to go back in there now?"

"Yes, I— That is, no."

"Okay, then, we'll come back when everything's working. For now, let's grab the elevator to the nineteenth floor." He motioned her to walk ahead. She did, tentatively, still anxious, he noticed, darting glances over her shoulder.

As they waited for the elevator, quietly, side by side, she seemed to relax a little, but there was still a tenseness in the way she held herself. Was she edgy about being alone with him in the subbasement, or was she actually afraid of him? He hoped it wasn't that. He wanted her to trust him, but he had to admit that the circumstances of both their meetings had sinister overtones.

She smiled nervously at him, and Will was reminded of how damned good-looking she was. Her honey-colored hair was short and curly, and even her skin had a golden sheen. Her eyes were the clearest blue he'd ever seen. They were the kind of eyes that reflected everything she was thinking, guileless eyes that couldn't lie, blue, blue eyes that a man could get lost in.

"I hear the elevator coming now," he assured her. "It shouldn't be much longer." Almost as soon as he spoke, it arrived, and the door slid open.

Kasey breathed deeply after they got in and the car began to move upward. "Now if we can make it to nineteen," she joked.

"Every day's an adventure at Bartow Tower," he said lightly. This time she smiled without anxiety, looking at him across the confines of the car; it was the speculative, even intimate gaze of a woman who had shared a brief, if artificial, closeness with a man.

Suddenly, vividly, the sensory memory of being close to her in the darkness enveloped Will. He remembered the warmth that emanated from her body through the gate, the scent of her freshly shampooed hair, the aroma of her perfume.

Then he thought of the rest of the day, and night, that stretched before him. He didn't look forward to spending it alone, shut away from the world. Hiding.

"Would you like to go out to dinner tonight?" He surprised himself by blurting out the invitation.

Her blue eyes widened in surprise. "Dinner?"

She seemed confused, and he didn't blame her. As far as she was concerned, the invitation came out of the blue. She didn't know that he'd been thinking about her since the elevator incident, wondering when he would see her again.

"Just a thought," he added quickly.

"That's very kind, but I work nights."

"Every night?" He quirked an unbelieving eyebrow.

"Yes, until the manager gets back from vacation." Her face was ingenuous, and her eyes met his evenly. "Maybe another time," she said politely as they reached their floor and stepped into the hallway. "Dinner sounds nice."

Nice. His mouth curled sardonically. It wasn't a word usually associated with him. "Maybe so," he replied.

She stood for a moment as if unsure of what to say next. "Well," she finally managed to say, "so long, Will." She moved to her door and fumbled with the keys. He thought about calling out to her and inviting her for Saturday or Sunday lunch. Then he caught himself. It was best to let well enough alone.

MUCH LATER that evening, around midnight, Will pushed himself away from the computer, stood up, stretched and poured a glass of brandy. He opened the balcony doors and stepped into the night air. The city lay before him, still wrapped in lights even at this late hour. The air had cooled and there was a faint breeze blowing.

He felt an unexpected wave of loneliness. It hit him hard. How was it possible, he wondered, in a city of more than ten million people, to feel so alone? Easy. It had been a long time since he'd had a decent conversation, shared a meal or talked late into the night with another person. The only one he knew in the building, other than the doorman and superintendent, was the woman next door, Kasey Halliday with deep blue eyes and a swirl of blond hair. Vulnerable, appealing. He'd tried before not to think of her. It hadn't been possible then; it wasn't now.

He took a swig of brandy, savoring the rich mellow flavor. It was expensive, but tonight that was no comfort. Drinking alone wasn't a good sign, and it wasn't what he wanted.

Maybe it was just as well that Kasey had turned down his dinner invitation. It would be dangerous for him to get involved with anyone now. He'd been crazy to spout off about fate throwing them together and even crazier to ask her out. He shrugged. What the hell; even though he didn't believe in fate for a moment, it was a good line.

Not that she'd fallen for it. She'd been edgy and skittish as if sensing something dangerous about him. He downed the brandy, went inside and poured another one. The night was long, and the darkness seemed to stretch endlessly before him.

KASEY WOKE UP at seven on Saturday morning, looked at the clock and turned over, closing her eyes. Why was she awake so early? She'd gotten home late the night before and had expected to sleep in. It hadn't worked. Something was the matter. She was keyed up, unable to relax.

Maybe it was the stress of her new job . . . or concern about Carl. Or maybe it was those recent adventures with her new neighbor. Whatever it was, getting back to sleep was impossible now. The morning shimmered with heat. She lay in bed and watched hazy sunlight sneak through the slits in her bedroom blinds. She could almost feel the rays. It was going to be another sizzler.

She rolled out of bed, pulled on a pair of shorts, slipped into her sneakers and searched for a T-shirt. She tossed aside her favorite, the black *Phantom of the Opera* shirt, remembering that dark colors attracted the sun, and chose a white one decorated with the logo of Walk-by-Windows. She planned to be outside today, walking off restless energy.

Other New Yorkers weren't as eager as she was to get out of their air-conditioned apartments, Kasey realized as she walked along a strangely deserted West Seventy-second Street. There wasn't even an early-morning jogger or a person walking a dog to share her solitude. It wasn't unusual for her neighborhood to be uncrowded on a summer weekend morning. Anyone who could afford it left the city, and those remaining stayed inside. But this morning, the street was more than uncrowded—it was totally empty.

A car cruised slowly by, then picked up speed. Kasey instinctively moved away from the curb and closer to the buildings, dodging trash cans, skirting the porch steps of old brownstone homes and the awnings of renovated apartment buildings.

Kasey's footsteps, even in her sneakers, seemed to echo between the tall canyons of concrete, steel and stone. She looked over her shoulder frequently. That had become a habit recently when she was out at night. Now she was doing it in daytime. She realized she was being a little irrational. There was no reason to feel unsafe on this peaceful Saturday morning, she told herself.

But suddenly, she felt the impersonality of the city more than ever; it overwhelmed her. For a brief moment, she was overcome by a fantasy that she was the only person left alive in New York. Totally alone. She quickened her steps and hit Broadway almost at a run.

When she reached the newsstand, Mike had her paper folded and waiting. "Hey there, Kasey," he said. "It's gonna be a scorcher. Two degrees up from yesterday, I predict."

Mike had a daily comment on every change in the weather. This morning, Kasey responded more agreeably than usual and even hung around for a few moments to chat about the heat. Then, crossing Broadway toward the bakery, she noticed that the city was finally coming to life, filling with pedestrians on their way out for coffee and morning newspapers.

Fenelli's smelled wonderful, as always, the aroma of just-baked bread mixing with that of freshly brewed coffee. Gina Fenelli was working the counter, waiting on a customer and extolling the virtues of her newest grandchild. Kasey gave her a wave before perusing the pastries, thoughtfully, her face close to the glass cases. Usually, she bought a single cheese danish. But what she craved today was a half-dozen kinds of wonderful, flaky delicacies—and someone to share them with.

She thought of Will Eastman. He was alone in the city, too. Right next door to her. They'd been locked in close quarters together twice with no ill effects, once in total darkness. He'd even asked her to have dinner with him. Going out with Will at night might have been risky, even if it had been possible. But now, in the bright morning sunshine . . .

"The usual, Kasey, a nice cheese danish?" Gina asked.

Before she had a chance to change her mind, Kasey impulsively ordered. "No, I'd like a mixture today. One cheese, one apricot, an almond croissant, a cinnamon twist and a . . . chocolate croissant. A half-dozen to go, please."

"That's only five, Kasey. One more."

"How about something special. Elegant."

Gina quickly reached under the glass counter. "Raspberry hazelnut torte. Very special." She looked at Kasey speculatively. "So you've got company?" Happily married, with four children and twice as many grandchildren, Gina worried about Kasey's single status.

"Not company. Just sharing with a neighbor. Maybe."

Gina bagged the pastries. "You never know, dear. You always have to be prepared for the unexpected."

That was certainly true, Kasey thought as she walked toward her building. The unexpected had already happened when she got stranded twice with Will. What had Will called it? Fate. Kasey liked the sound of that, but she still wasn't sure if knocking on Will's door on a Saturday morning with a bagful of pastries wasn't pushing fate too far.

He might not be there—or he might not be alone. Okay, she decided. That would be embarrassing, but it would end things then and there. On the other hand, if he was there—and alone—there would be no harm in offering to share the West Side's best pastries with him. It would be neighborly. Or was she asking for trouble?

Kasey slowed down as she approached Bartow Tower, and tried to analyze her feelings about Will Eastman. He was certainly attractive. No, he was more than that. Handsome. Sexy. A hunk. But there was something else, something she couldn't put her finger on. Beyond the charm and wit, there was a wariness, an edge.

She was curious as hell about him.

The night before, she'd made the mistake of telling Judy about being locked in the subbasement with Will. For a while, Judy's imagination had run amok. She'd attempted to connect Will and Carl, implying that Carl could have hired Kasey's neighbor to harass her.

Kasey had burst into laughter over that complex scenario. Carl and Will were light-years apart; there was no way the two men could know each other.

Besides, Will hadn't harassed her. She'd been the bad guy, the one who'd created the problem yesterday, practically knocking him down with the door and then locking him in the storage area. After he got out, he'd been very polite and had even asked her to dinner.

Confused thoughts about Will dashed wildly around in her head as she breezed past Tim with a wave and grabbed the elevator.

Judy was right. In spite of their two encounters, he was still a stranger. There were plenty of crazies out there, Judy had been fast to warn her, who seemed perfectly normal most of the time, until one day, out of the blue, they became monsters.

"Monsters!" Kasey said aloud as she stepped off on the nineteenth floor. "Ridiculous." He was just her neighbor, an intriguing man with whom she was about to share her breakfast. She headed toward his door. Sometimes a woman could be so damned careful that she missed out on life. She rang the bell of apartment 1905.

Nothing happened. She rang again and waited. After a minute or so, her optimism began to sputter and fail. Nothing lost, she decided. She would take the pastries to her apartment, make a pot of coffee and pig out.

The door opened. Kasey's eyes widened. Her heart gave a disconcerting flutter as she was confronted by a broad bare chest, well-muscled legs, dark hair and beard shimmering with drops of water on a body that was bronzed, gorgeous and nude. Except for a towel that barely covered his hips. She didn't know where to look. Up. That was safe.

Her gaze met smiling eyes. She took a step backward and held up the bakery bag. "Pastries. I was on my way back from the bakery and..."

Will looked down at her for a moment, the twinkle still in his eyes, his head cocked to one side. She had no idea what he was thinking.

Then he waved her in. "Good timing. I have a pot of coffee brewing. Why don't you wait on the balcony and I'll get dressed."

Kasey stepped inside before she had a chance to change her mind and then headed down the narrow hallway toward the balcony. The layout of all Bartow Tower one-bedroom apartments was the same, so she moved quickly and easily past the bedroom and bath, across the living room, where sunlight streamed in through the balcony doors.

Will followed her, seemingly unperturbed about his state of undress, apologizing instead about the cluttered apartment. "Sorry for the mess." They threaded through piles of books and stacks of papers and magazines. "I'm still unpacking," he explained easily.

She tried to concentrate on the room and not on the man as he moved beside her, holding the towel in place. But any woman with an ounce of red blood would have had trouble avoiding that body. The flat hard muscles of his chest and abdomen, the feathering of dark hair that drifted down his chest and continued in a narrow line before disappearing under the towel, and the long lean muscles of his legs.

She looked away, noticed a computer, laser printer and a stack of disks—an entire office set up in the corner—and managed to focus on them. "At least you have your work space arranged," she said.

His answer was to usher her firmly toward the outside doors. "I'll be back in a couple of minutes with coffee. Enjoy the view. It should be familiar," he added with a grin.

Kasey watched as he closed the doors behind him. Clearly, he was a man serious about his privacy. She couldn't blame him. After all, she was an unexpected guest. And she felt sure that Will wasn't the type to open his life to anyone.

The balcony was a perfect setting for breakfast, with a wrought-iron glass-topped table and matching chairs. Jim's array of potted plants bloomed profusely, as usual. She'd noticed that through the spring and early summer. Whereas, only a few feet away on her own balcony, her pitiful plants languished unhappily. This was by far a more interesting balcony, which was probably why Lo Mein visited so often.

She sat down at the table, opened her bag of pastries and spread them on napkins as Will appeared, carrying two cups of coffee. He wore shorts and a T-shirt.

"What a great shirt," she said. It was brilliant chartreuse with the bright purple outline of a huge eye staring at her. A little unnerving, slightly eerie, but definitely original. "I'm a nut for unusual T-shirts." She looked down at her own. "I don't often resort to ones that advertise the restaurant where I work."

He handed her a cup of steaming coffee and let his eyes take in her shirt. "It's an interesting logo," he said casually. "Mine was last year's birthday present from a friend. I brought it out to celebrate the occasion."

"Today's your birthday?"

She thought he nodded but couldn't be sure as he sat down at the table, ignored the torte and chose the chocolate croissant. "Hmm. Great. I love chocolate. My compliments to the chef."

"Thanks. The name's Fenelli and the bakery's across Broadway... But you didn't answer. Is today your birthday?"

"Guilty," he admitted.

"And you asked me to dinner last night to celebrate? Now I feel terrible that I couldn't go." At the same time, she wondered why a man as attractive as Will had no one to share his birthday with.

His mouth curved in a smile. "You could have quit your job and come with me."

Kasey took a bite of the cinnamon twist and shook her head. "I wouldn't go so far as to quit my job, but I'm glad I gave in to the impulse to buy a few extra pastries and share breakfast with you." She held up her coffee cup in a toast. "Happy birthday!"

"Thanks." He looked at her over the rim of his cup. The gaze was so intense that it caused a little shiver to travel down Kasey's spine despite the heat of the sun. "Are you always so impetuous, Kasey?" he asked.

"Most of the time," she admitted. "It's a very bad trait, I'm told. My friend Judy says—" Kasey broke off and settled back in her chair, her arms crossed determinedly. "Oh, no, Will Eastman. Not this time. I go on and on about my life while you remain mysterious about yours."

He examined the pastries. "This one looks good."

"Raspberry hazelnut torte."

"Great choice." He took a big bite.

"But you're not going to tell me about yourself," she probed. "No fair."

He leaned back in his chair. "Life isn't fair, Kasey. Haven't you learned that?"

She was surprised by the bitterness in his words, but he didn't stop for her to comment.

"Since you wouldn't have dinner with me—"

"*Couldn't*," she corrected.

"Since you couldn't have dinner last night, what about tonight?"

"Work. Remember?"

"Even on the weekend?"

"Especially on the weekend, at least while my boss is out of town."

"What about a late dinner?"

Kasey laughed. "That would be pretty late!"

"I don't mind if you don't."

"All the good restaurants would be closed," she told him. "But I have an idea. We could have lunch in the park."

A fleeting unreadable look flickered across his face. He shook his head.

"Why not?" she asked

"Not during the day," he said, adding quickly, "It's too hot."

"It'll be cool by the lake, and the city's practically deserted, so we'd have Central Park almost to ourselves. We could stop at a deli, or even better, buy hot dogs in the park, with sauerkraut, mustard and onions—and an orange drink. And fries!" She was warming to the idea of lunch before she'd even finished breakfast.

Will laughed but didn't seem convinced. "It's a long, hot walk to the lake."

"Then we'll take a taxi." She took a bite of the cinnamon twist.

"You have all the answers." He leaned across the table and touched her lips with his napkin. "Sugar," he explained.

Their faces were close. She could smell his warm soapy scent and see the flecks of gold in his dark eyes. Kasey felt something inside her tighten. It was a powerful, visceral—and totally sexual—reaction to Will's closeness.

Unable to unlock herself from his gaze, she pushed back her chair. At least that seemed to ease the tension between them. "So how about it?" she managed to say. "Shall we do it?"

His eyes challenged hers. "Do it, Kasey?" He raised his dark eyebrows.

"Have lunch in the park." Why couldn't she stop looking at him? It was impossible, that's why. The balcony was just too small. She would be much safer in the vastness of Central Park.

He looked away. She breathed a sigh and waited.

After a long moment, he gave a little shrug. "Why not? Let's eat hot dogs in the park and enjoy the sun. Meet you by the elevator at noon."

Kasey realized she was holding her breath. She let it out slowly. She and Will had just taken a big step in their unusual relationship. But was it a step in the right direction?

"I DON'T BELIEVE IT," Will said as they got out of the taxi in the middle of Central Park. "It's an oasis."

"Nope, just a lake."

"I've never seen this end of it," he told her.

Will followed Kasey toward the lake as a gondola pulled away from the dock. "Are we in New York or Venice?"

"Isn't it great? The gondola's authentic. All the way from Italy. And the boathouse has been turned into a restaurant.

"My guess is that we're not eating there."

Kasey laughed. "Not when we have our special hot dogs."

"And orange drinks," he added.

They crossed a wooden deck in front of the restaurant and went down the steps to a lush green knoll beside the lake. Kasey unfolded a red-and-white-checked tablecloth and they settled on the grass.

Looking around, Will commented, "You were right. The place is almost deserted."

"Everybody who *can* gets out of the city in August." Kasey passed Will a hot dog. "These are the best in the world, I'm told. 'Course, I've only been in Missouri and New York. I guess you've traveled a lot."

"A lot," he acknowledged, "but you've discovered a place I didn't even know existed." He took a big bite of his hot dog.

"What do you mean by 'a lot'?"

"Um?" he asked, his mouth full.

"What's 'a lot'? Europe? The Far East?"

"Um. Both," he said, taking another bite.

"You're impossible," Kasey chided. "Every time I ask a question, you eat! Why won't you talk about yourself? Stop," she warned with a laugh, "don't take another bite of that hot dog!"

Will grinned. "Can I have a swig of my orange drink?"

"Okay," she agreed. "If you'll tell me about yourself then. After all, we're neighbors."

"And that means we tell all? You have a very interesting way of looking at life, Kasey."

"Everyone tells me that I'm too open, but there're worse things in life."

"Maybe," Will replied. "But this is New York City, not a small town. Things are different here."

"But I'm the same, Will. I'm always friendly and outgoing. Too trusting, I guess. And you're the way you are."

Will took another long swig of his drink, pulled off his sunglasses and lay back on the grass. He put his hands behind his head and closed his eyes. Kasey couldn't help noticing how the movement delineated his chest and shoulder muscles under his T-shirt. "And how *am* I, Kasey?"

"Secretive and mysterious."

"Secretive and mysterious," he repeated. "Maybe I should dispel that image." He opened his eyes and squinted a little as he looked over at her. "By giving you a brief résumé. I was born in Vermont thirty years ago. Went to college in the East. Got married. Got divorced. No children. In New York to start a new life."

"A new life," she repeated. "How?"

Will laughed. "You don't give up, do you? Well, maybe I'll get a job. It shouldn't be too difficult since I've done just about everything from bartender to cabdriver to construction worker..." He closed his eyes again.

Kasey finished her hot dog and watched him as he lay there quietly, seemingly so relaxed. *Sophisticated* and *stylish* were words that came to mind. Not *bartender* or *taxi driver*. She remembered his apartment with its top-of-the-line computer system. The thought of Will as an ordinary worker didn't seem to fit, especially since she'd seen his very expensive, far from blue-collar, clothes.

I guess you use your computer for résumés," she commented.

"Mmm. Sometimes. Among other things."

Since he was being evasive again, Kasey tried another tack. "Well, if things get really tough for you, we might be able to use an extra bartender at Windows."

He opened one eye, squinting again. Was he grateful—or amused? she wondered. She couldn't tell.

"Thanks," he said simply. "I'll keep that in mind. Actually, I'm onto something now that may work out."

Kasey stood, put their paper plates and cups in the trash and leaned back against a tree near Will, wishing she had the nerve to stretch out beside him. Just for the fun of it, she let herself fantasize about what that would be like, lying next to Will, her head on his shoulder, relaxed, happy, while listening to his soft breathing and feeling the warmth of his body.

"So, what brought you to New York?" he asked, jolting Kasey from her fantasy.

She took a moment to recover. "I came with someone else—my boyfriend, actually."

Will raised one dark eyebrow as Kasey continued, "He wanted to give the big city a try. He hated it. I loved it. He tried to adapt for my sake, but that just made us both miserable. So he left and I began looking for a job. The only one I could get before my money ran out was waitressing at Windows. There," she said, "ask me a simple question, and I give a very complete answer, don't I?"

"That's very refreshing." Will rolled over on one elbow so that he was looking at her. "You worked yourself up at the restaurant, so you must like the job."

"I love it. The people who work there are special." She rethought that remark and added, "Most of them are, anyway. They're like family."

Will idly plucked a blade of grass. "Let's see if I can figure out your background." He chewed on the grass thoughtfully. "Large family. You're the middle child. There was always a lot going on, and you miss all the activity."

"That's true, I do."

"Really? Did I get it right?" he asked.

Kasey laughed. "Well, I do miss the activity, but it didn't come from a big family." Kasey smiled at him. "I'm an only child, born to middle-aged parents. Our house always seemed very lonely so I created my own excitement. My own extended family."

At Will's puzzled frown, she said, "No, I didn't dream them up. Well, maybe some of the time," she added. "I was the kind of kid who went all around the neighborhood, pushing myself into everyone's life. My whole hometown was my family."

He stroked his beard. "And they all loved you. Which is what you wanted."

"Is there a charge for the psychotherapy, Doctor? Oh, I don't mind," she insisted when he started to apologize. "I admit that I do like to be liked, and I reach out to people, who usually respond. What's wrong with that?"

"Nothing. Just so you know that everyone in the world isn't a nice guy."

"Of course I do. I'm friendly, not stupid." She thought of Carl again, but quickly dismissed the image. "Most people respond positively if you give them a chance."

"Interesting philosophy," Will said.

"But you disagree."

He shrugged.

"Another item added to in the list of things we *don't* have in common."

"Maybe. But here's one we share—I'm also an only child."

"Really? Did you hate it, too?"

Will grinned, his golden-brown eyes sparkling. "I thought it was great. All the attention, all the presents—just for me. Obviously I'm more selfish than you. Another difference between us," he teased.

Kasey realized that he was totally relaxed, as relaxed as she had ever seen him. She'd love to linger there beside him all day, ticking off what they didn't—or did—have in common.

"We better be heading back," he said.

Well, so much for that idea, Kasey thought as she folded the tablecloth. She wasn't sure why he needed to get back, but she refrained from asking any more questions.

Will got to his feet, stretched his arms high above his head and then held out his hand to her. "Thanks for the picnic. This has been a nice break for me."

She took his hand, which was warm and firm, and she didn't let go. What harm could there be in holding hands for a little while? "I enjoyed myself, too." She laughed. "We have that in common. Maybe we can do it again."

"Maybe."

Hardly a resounding response, Kasey thought, still pleased that he held on to her hand as they climbed the stairs and crossed the deck.

"Want to walk back?" she asked.

"Nope, let's grab a taxi."

When they reached the street, Kasey noticed that a breeze had come up, bringing with it a flurry of activity. Kids sped by on inline skates and a group of late lunchers spilled from a taxi and headed for the restaurant.

Will flagged down a taxi, which pulled up at the curb beside them. As he reached for the door, Kasey heard someone call out. She looked toward the restaurant to see a man raise his hand in greeting. Kasey didn't recognize him.

She tugged on Will's arm. "Someone over there seems to know you."

Will glanced around quickly and then hurried Kasey into the taxi. Before she could look again, Will was on the seat beside her, giving the driver their address.

"I think he called your name," she said.

"Not me," he replied brusquely. "I've never seen that guy in my life."

4

THEIR TAXI TURNED onto Seventy-second Street and came to a dead stop.

"What's going on?" Will asked.

"Problem up ahead. Looks like a fire truck in the street," the cabbie replied casually.

"Oh, no," Kasey cried. "Is it Bartow Tower?"

"You mean Bartow Horror?" The cabbie laughed. "From what I hear, putting a match to that place would be a good idea." He leaned out the window. "Hey, wait a minute. There are a couple of cop cars up ahead."

Will pulled some bills out of his wallet and shoved them toward the driver. "We'll walk the rest of the way," he said as Kasey opened the door and got out.

"I don't see any smoke," she told Will.

"Probably just another computer failure."

"I hope that's all it is," Kasey said, rushing along the sidewalk beside Will.

"It's not a fire," he assured her.

Then Kasey saw the television van. "Something terrible must have happened!" She moved ahead of him. "There's Marge Durant—from the tenants' association."

Marge, stocky, red-faced and flustered, rushed up to them. "Kasey, we tried to call you earlier to help us get the pickets organized."

"What happened?"

"Two kids got stuck in an elevator. They shouldn't have been in there alone, if you ask me. They're not even old enough to go to school yet. Oh, hi," she said to Will, holding out her freckled hand. "I'm Marge."

Will shook her hand without introducing himself, which didn't stop Marge from babbling on. "Can you believe this? They call Bartow a luxury high rise. It's less than two years old, complete with a high-tech computer, which is the problem, if you ask me—"

"Marge," Kasey interrupted. "Finish explaining what happened."

"Oh, the kids' parents panicked and called the fire department. They got them out, but the whole thing took nearly an hour, and the parents were hysterical. Meanwhile, the police came—and now this!" She gestured toward the commotion that included the fire truck, two police cars and a news van.

"Television cameras—for a stuck elevator?" Kasey was incredulous.

"Must be a slow news day," Marge responded. "But it's great for us. They're interviewing everyone who has a horror story about the building." Her round face was glowing with perspiration and excitement. "This is just the kind of exposure we need to get the story out about Bartow."

"It's already out," Kasey said. "Our driver knew the Bartow Horror nickname. Remember, Will?"

She turned around, toward where Will had been standing.

"Looking for that tall, dark and handsome hunk, if someone my age can use such an expression?" Marge asked.

"Will Eastman. He's subletting on my floor."

"And he's vanished in a puff of smoke."

"That's so weird," Kasey said, trying not to feel hurt.

"You two got something going?" Marge asked bluntly.

"Good Lord, no, Marge. We met in a stuck elevator," she said lightly. "But he was really livid about it. You'd think he would be concerned that it's happened again so soon. You'd think he would want to—"

"Maybe he's publicity-shy. He beat it out of here as soon as the TV cameras pointed this way."

"Oh, Marge, I'm sure that didn't have anything to do with his leaving. Still . . ." Her voice trailed off.

"Well, whatever. You have a story, so let's get it out." She yelled toward the television news van. "Yoo-hoo, over here, Kasey Halliday has firsthand experience with the Bartow Horror elevators!"

KASEY SAT at her desk at the restaurant, deliberately ignoring the stack of invoices piled up before her. In the small, windowless room, her thoughts seemed to bounce off the walls and back to her in boomerang fashion. And all of them were about the same subject. Will Eastman.

Two days had passed since their afternoon together. They'd got to know each other a little, casually. Well, more than casually, Kasey admitted. She'd revealed a lot about herself, and he'd done the same, although somewhat reluctantly.

His vanishing act a little later had thrown her off-balance completely. One moment he was there beside her, the next he was gone.

Several times since then, she'd thought about knocking on his door and asking him for an explanation, but she hadn't. Pride held her back. Besides, it wasn't really any of her business. Will was free to come and go as he pleased. And if his comings and goings included disappearing during a date of sorts, that was his prerogative.

She closed her eyes, cleared her head, then opened her eyes and attacked the invoices again, giving special attention to one from the fish market, a whopper that would put them well over budget before the end of the month. She set it aside and made a note to talk to the chef about it. What was Albert trying to do, start his own lobster farm? Gritting her teeth, Kasey picked up the next invoice.

"So how's the TV star this morning?" Judy stood in the doorway.

"Just like I was yesterday—totally unknown."

"Ha! No way," Judy said as she dropped into the chair beside Kasey's desk. "Mom called last night and said Aunt Irene from New Jersey caught you on the eleven o'clock news Sunday night and the early show Monday morning."

Kasey was nonplussed.

"Irene watches TV at least eighteen hours a day. But she didn't record it for me. Neither did Mom. Let's face it. They don't have a clue about working a VCR."

"I should have recorded it," Kasey said. "I guess. But I never thought . . ." Her words drifted off. "I suppose there were other things on my mind."

"Other things? That sounds interesting. And mysterious. Who? What?"

Kasey chewed indecisively on her lower lip. She wanted to talk to Judy about Will, but she knew what her friend's reaction would be: more warnings, more I-told-you-so's. But she still needed someone else's perspective.

"Kasey, I know something's going on in that head of yours. So tell me."

Kasey took a deep breath and launched into her story, beginning with the pastries and ending with the TV cameras.

"So he vanished into thin air?"

"Seemed like it to me. One moment he was there, the next, poof!"

"And you haven't heard from him? No phone call telling you how much he enjoyed the day?"

Kasey shook her head.

"No bouquet of flowers apologizing for his behavior?"

Kasey laughed. "Well, I didn't expect flowers, but I did expect some kind of explanation, especially since we had such a good time. I can't figure out what happened."

"I can." Judy leaned forward, her voice low and conspiratorial. "Think about it, Kasey. When did he disappear? I'll tell you when," she responded to her own question. "He left as soon as he saw the cameras turned in his direction. And do you know why?"

"No, but I'm sure you'll tell me," Kasey answered with a sigh.

"I sure will. He's hiding out."

"What? Hiding out! Are you trying to say he's a fugitive? Judy, that's ridiculous. If you knew him—"

"Well, I don't know him, but I doubt he's hiding from the law. More likely, he's hiding from his wife." She sat back in her chair and folded her arms. "Case solved."

Kasey shook her head. "Sorry to tell you this, but he's divorced."

"Okay. No problem. He's hiding from his ex-wife. Probably owes back alimony."

"Judy, you've got a great imagination," Kasey said with a laugh.

"Not imagination. Logic. I'm being logical, and you're being—I might as well say it—gullible. Especially if you believe everything told to you by this married man with a crazy wife."

"Oh, now he's married again. And with a crazy wife! You're too much, Judy."

"Maybe. But at least I'm not hung up on a total stranger."

"He lives next door," Kasey reminded her friend. "Besides, he's the most interesting man I've ever met—"

"Up until now," Judy said, finishing for her. "That's gonna change because Danny and I are having a party. And if anyone has interesting friends, it's *my* boyfriend."

"A party? When?" Kasey asked.

"Well, soon. It'll be soon. Next week."

Kasey shook her head in wonder. "You just came up with the idea to have a party now, didn't you?"

"Maybe." Judy laughed. "But it's a good idea. I'll give you all the details as soon as I know them," she said with a giggle. "After I talk to Danny." Judy stood up, glancing at her watch. "Time for me to get back. Some of us have to work around here even if management goofs off, lost in secret fantasies about the man next door."

Kasey threw up her hands in defeat. "Okay, no more fantasies. He's totally out of my mind, and that's where he'll stay."

"Sure. And if you keep telling stories like that, your nose will grow, Pinocchio."

Kasey made a face at her friend's retreating back. Judy knew her all too well.

KASEY WAS PLEASED with the way the evening was going. She was having a hell of a lot of fun and gaining more and more confidence in her position as acting manager. She felt as if the restaurant were hers, and it was a damned good feeling.

Doing what she did best and enjoyed the most, Kasey circulated, talking to customers, basking in compliments. The world seemed to like Windows. She didn't blame them.

When Judy approached with a dark expression on her face, Kasey braced herself. It looked bad, but she could handle it.

The first words out of Judy's mouth confirmed the bad part. "We got trouble, pal."

"What is it?" Then she panicked. "Carl's back!"

"No. Not Carl. Someone even more intimidating."

Kasey looked blank. "I give up."

Lowering her voice, Judy said, "I'm about to speak two words that will put the fear of God in you. If not, you're made of steel."

"Enough teasing," Kasey scolded.

"Mattison Monroe."

For a moment, Kasey didn't move. Then she felt her legs go wobbly.

"Don't faint, for God's sake," Judy cried.

"I'm not going to faint. At least I don't think so. Where is he?"

"Section three. By the side windows. He's with a woman, his wife, probably. I've never seen a picture of her, but she's just about as huge as Mattison. A definite eater."

Kasey knew that every restaurant's greatest hope— and greatest fear—was for the top food critic in town to walk through the door. Kasey, holding on to Judy's hand, strolled around the restaurant, until she was directly across the room from Mattison Monroe. Not looking in his direction, she asked, "What did he order?"

"That's the problem, Kasey. He wants that new lobster dish that Albert's been working on."

"How did he find out about that? It's n-not even on the menu yet," Kasey stammered.

"Word gets out."

"Probably because of Albert's gargantuan lobster order. The bill is staggering."

"I hear he's gone through most of it coming up with the new dish. Lobster Albert, he calls it, of course."

Kasey headed for the kitchen with Judy in tow, pushed through the door and found Albert at his cutting board, expertly taking apart a whole chicken in a few quick motions.

"Albert—"

"No problem, Kasey," the round little Frenchman said, stopping long enough to wipe his hands on his splattered apron. "The lobster, she is on 'is plate, heading for 'is belly. Is no problem."

"You haven't even tried it on the staff yet, Albert. You can't serve it to New York's most powerful food critic. You can't, not yet!"

"The lobster, she—"

"Is on his plate," Judy repeated with the chef as Kasey turned and walked out of the kitchen, mumbling to herself.

"And I'm going to stop it. Now."

Judy caught up with her. "Maybe it'll be okay, Kasey. After all, he's been working on the recipe for days."

"He should have refused. It's not on the menu yet."

Judy opened the door and grabbed Kasey's arm. "It's also not on the table yet. Look, Kasey, you can stop it. The waiter hasn't served him. It's your call now."

They rushed to the waiter's station, right to the plate that held the questionable lobster. "Good Lord, Kasey. Check out that presentation. Get a whiff of that sauce."

Kasey leaned over and let the aroma envelop her. Then she stood up straight and waved the waiter on. "Go ahead, serve this masterpiece to the great man. I trust Albert, and if it tastes as good as it smells, we're home free."

She'd made the decision. There was nothing to do now but wait.

Kasey and Judy went through the paces of their jobs for the next hour, sneaking occasional glances at Mattison as he and his wife finished their meals, ordered coffee and brandy and lingered until nearly closing time. After the critic and his wife had left the restaurant, the two women heaved collective sighs, and exchanged hopeful hugs.

"I'm outta here," Judy said. "Date with Danny. Besides, I can't take any more tension."

"Oh, great. You're leaving the rest to me."

"You're the boss, Boss," Judy said as she headed for the door.

Kasey turned back, determined to finish the evening calmly. She stopped by the kitchen to give a thumbs-up to Albert, who was confidence personified. On her way back, the bartender stepped out of the lounge and waved to her. "You got a call in here. It's the boss."

"Fred," Kasey said to herself. Could news possibly travel that fast?

She skittered into the bar and picked up the phone. "Fred, I can't believe it! Your timing is perfect. Mattison Monroe just left."

There was a long silence while Kasey imagined Fred picking himself up off the floor. Then she told him the whole story.

"And you decided to let the dish go to the man."

"Yep. Was I wrong?"

Fred laughed. "We'll see."

"Fred—"

"No, of course not, Kasey. It was your decision. I trust you completely."

That response was followed by a long pause, which left Kasey puzzled. "Fred," she said softly, "what's the matter. What is it?"

"Nothing about Mattison. Nothing about your work," he said quickly. "But . . ."

"Fred," she prompted again.

"Okay, I'm going to come right out with it," he said, causing her anxiety level to rise. "I didn't want to tell you about this, but my wife insisted."

Kasey held her breath.

"I called home for my messages, and I had a weird one, Kasey. From Carl Dandridge."

Her fingers tightened on the receiver. "Carl?"

"Yep. I might as well tell you, it was an ugly call. The man sounded crazed, insisting I fire you and hire him back. I don't think he's a real threat, but you need to know how he reacted."

"I know already. He came by and made his threats in person. I didn't pay much attention," she added, not quite truthfully.

"He's just blowing off steam, but I want you to watch your step, just in case."

"I will."

"I chose you for the job because you get along with everyone," Fred told her. "Even Carl. That's what mystifies me about his taking his anger out on you, of all people."

"He holds me responsible for his failures, but I don't think he's dangerous."

"I don't, either, but be careful just the same. Look out for yourself."

"I will," she promised.

"Then I'll see you in a few days. What would you like as a memento of my vacation in Maine? How about a lobster?" he asked, chuckling at his own joke.

"At the rate Albert's going, that's not a bad idea."

LOOK OUT FOR YOURSELF. Fred's words rang in Kasey's head as she closed the restaurant for the night. It was the manager's job to shut the place down, lock the day's earnings in the safe, turn off the lights and set the alarm. Whenever the task fell to Kasey, she asked someone to stay with her. Tonight of all nights, she'd simply forgotten.

Judy had left early to go out with her boyfriend, and somehow the bartender and waiters had got away before Kasey. Even the late-night busboy had left early, and he was usually her self-appointed protector.

After Kasey set the locks and the burglar alarm, she went out the back door, mumbling to herself all the while. "Doesn't make sense. Leaving through the back. Ridiculous. Not to mention damned dangerous." Fred had set up the security system that way, but she was going to talk to him about it when he got back.

She was still mumbling as she looked both ways, checked to make sure there was no one lurking in the alley and then hurried out the gate toward the street. She stopped once, looked over her shoulder, just to assure herself there really wasn't anyone following her and then made a final bolt out into Columbus Circle.

The late-night crowd was louder and more boisterous than usual. She had to sidestep a drunk coming out of the corner bar, and as she crossed the street a sports car filled with teenagers skidded by, barely missing her. She rushed along, keeping a lookout for a taxi. She wasn't anxious to walk home alone.

But the heavy traffic didn't include any empty cabs. She could take the subway, Kasey thought; it was only one stop on the local. But the idea of going down the steps to the train never had been appealing, especially at night. Lurking in a subway station seemed like something Carl would do.

Carl. Kasey realized then that she'd been running from him ever since she left the restaurant. He'd threatened her twice—face-to-face and on Frank's answering machine. How did she know that he wouldn't follow her, with more than threats on his demented mind?

Kasey stepped out into the street, hand extended hopefully to flag down a taxi. The light changed, stopping all the traffic traveling uptown. She waited patiently and then began to wave as the light turned green and the cars sped past. "Damn," she said. "Guess I'm walking." She made her way across Columbus Circle, dodging traffic that didn't include any empty cabs.

As she headed toward her Upper West Side neighborhood and away from the late-night activity, the traffic thinned out. Soon, only an occasional car passed, its headlights casting eerie shadows against the buildings.

Kasey was still two blocks away from home, when she heard footsteps behind her. She turned around, quickly, expecting to see someone out for an evening walk. But no one was there. The street was deserted. She moved on, more slowly, taking careful, nearly silent steps.

Then she heard the footsteps again. They weren't echoes of her own, and they certainly weren't imaginary. She sped up; the footsteps moved just as quickly. Still moving forward, she glanced around once more, and that's when she saw him, a dark, shadowy figure, barely discernible. Kasey began to run.

Across the street, a young couple had just got into their car. She rushed toward them, about to ask for help, when they drove off, laughing and gesturing toward her.

When she'd crossed the street, the man behind her had followed. Now he was closer, almost upon her.

Her heart pounded, and she moved faster, struggling to catch her breath. Judy and Fred were right. Carl Dandridge was a dangerous man, and he was after her! She could hear his footsteps coming closer and closer. Then he called out her name.

"Kasey, stop, Kasey!" The voice sounded muffled in the heavy night air.

Did he think she was insane? Did he think she'd stop for him on a nearly deserted street just because he'd called her name? She reached inside for her last reserve of energy, but he was gaining on her. The faster she ran, the quicker he closed the gap. She imagined she could even feel his breath on her neck; he seemed that close. And he was!

She let out a yell as his hand touched her shoulder.

"No!" she cried, whirling and crouching in a defensive position, her best imitation of a karate stance.

He was wearing a dark shirt and trousers, and his face was half-hidden in the shadows. "Don't touch me or—" She broke off in midthreat when he stepped into the glow of the streetlight.

"Will?" She stood up, facing him, relieved.

"Yes. Why were you running, Kasey?"

"I didn't know it was you."

"I'm sorry for frightening you. I thought you would stop when I called your name."

"No, I thought you were—" She broke off, winded, trying to catch her breath.

"Who?" he asked.

"No one. Nothing." She didn't explain further as she pushed her hair back from her face and looked at him. "What are you doing here?" There was no hiding the suspicion in her voice.

"Taking a walk," he answered immediately. "I like to walk at night."

He was a night walker? Kasey thought of Glenna's facetious remark about Will as a vampire.

"You told me where you worked, remember? I knew that you got off late, and since I was nearby..." He shrugged. "I thought maybe I could walk you home."

She looked down the street. "I'm nearly there."

"I missed you at the restaurant. Then I saw you crossing Columbus Circle and tried to catch up. But you make good time, lady."

Kasey couldn't help smiling.

"May I walk you the rest of the way?"

There was just enough light for Kasey to see his bearded face. His eyes seemed honest, his voice sounded reasonable enough. She bit down on her lip and hesitated.

"Or we could have a drink at that little bar a couple of blocks back, and then I'll put you in a taxi," he said smoothly, "if that will make you feel safer."

Kasey sighed, aware that her anxiety must be easy for him to read. "No," she said. "It's too late for a drink, but I'd like for you to walk me the rest of the way home," she said firmly.

Will took her elbow and started to walk. "I have a confession," he said.

Kasey glanced at him out of the corner of her eye. "That sounds serious."

"An apology, actually. I want to say that I'm sorry for leaving you to face the television cameras on Saturday. The whole thing was too much for me. It seemed exploitative."

"Exploitative?" she asked.

"Of the children, the parents."

"Oh." Kasey was thoughtful. "That's certainly an unusual take. All this time I had another idea about your disappearance. I thought maybe you were running from the media."

"Really?" He didn't break stride, she noted, but even while he kept on walking, Kasey was pretty sure she felt his hand tighten and then relax on her arm. "How do you mean that?" he asked.

"Well, I thought you were running from the television cameras because someone might see you."

"An interesting theory," he commented casually. "Any other twists on it?"

They stopped at the corner, and the streetlight slanted across his face, leaving it shadowed. He looked at her quizzically, and Kasey knew she should just shrug and change the subject. That would probably please him. On the other hand, she could plunge ahead.

"Maybe you're in hiding," she ventured.

"In hiding, huh? Who from, the law?" He gave a half smile. "The light's with us, come on." As they walked, he looked down at her with the smile still on his lips. "I can swear to you unequivocally that I'm not running from the law. The cops aren't closing in on me, Kasey."

He'd succeeded in making her feel embarrassed about her question. "Well, of course not. I didn't really think they were. I guess I was just letting my imagination play games."

"That's called fantasizing, Kasey. And that makes me the object of your fantasy," he teased.

"No, I—"

"Just kidding," he said.

They were just a few doors from Bartow Tower, when she decided to go all the way with her thoughts.

"I also imagined—only for a minute—that maybe you didn't want your wife to see you on television."

"I don't have a wife," he said as they walked under the Bartow canopy and toward the front door. "I have an ex-wife."

When they reached the marble lobby, Tim looked up from his desk, his eyes lit with interest. "Well, well. Ms. Halliday and Mr. Eastman. Been out on the town?"

Kasey was determined to stop that rumor before it began. "I ran into Mr. Eastman on my way home from work," she said curtly.

"Small world, eh?"

"Very," Will replied, pushing the elevator button. "This one guaranteed to work tonight?"

"They were both checked out today. No problem," Tim assured them.

The door opened and they stepped inside. "I wouldn't mind, you know." Will folded his arms and leaned against the elevator wall, looking at her with that teasing half smile.

"Mind what?" Kasey asked.

"Getting stuck in the elevator again. With you. Now that we know each other." He reached for the panel of buttons.

"Don't you dare! We'd probably be here for days."

"Worse things have happened," he said with a grin. But he let the elevator come to a stop smoothly on the nineteenth floor.

Will walked Kasey to her door. "I'm glad I ran into you—or ran you down," he said. "And I hope you accept my apology for leaving you the other day."

"Of course. Not everyone wants to be on the front lines in the Bartow protest, or on television. I understand completely, even though I seem to head for the front lines myself," she added with a smile.

He brushed his fingers against her cheek. "You're quite a woman, Kasey. Amusing—" he cupped her chin "—but also thoughtful and caring. Dedicated."

Kasey's eyes widened at his touch. "No, I'm not really—"

"Sure you are. You care about your friends in the tenants' association. You work hard for your causes, your beliefs. I bet you care about everyone who lives in this building."

"Well . . ." She wasn't about to tell him of her reputation as the Bartow Tower housemother.

"Besides," he added, studying her face intently, "your eyes are the color of a summer sky."

The words came out of nowhere, and as he spoke them, he leaned down, his mouth close to hers. She closed her eyes and felt herself drawn to him.

His mouth grazed hers lightly. Kasey liked the feeling, the warmth, the softness. She opened her lips slightly, inviting more. Will responded by slipping his arms around her, pulling her to him.

Then he kissed her again, this time thoroughly, greedily. The intensity of his kiss jolted all her senses into instant awareness. His tongue touched hers and instinctively Kasey took it into her mouth. He probed the sensitive softness while Kasey tasted him, savored him.

She felt the hard muscles of his shoulders and chest against her, the strength of his arms around her. She drank in the tangy scent of his after-shave and ran her fingers through the crisp texture of his hair just above his collar. His beard was rough against her face, but his lips were cool, moist, tender—and urgent. There was infinite excitement in the unexpected contrast.

Kasey could feel the blood surging through her body, the growing heat of her skin, the warm tingling that spread inside her. When the kiss ended, he held on to her, cradling her against him. His breathing was as uneven as hers, the pounding of his heart as rapid.

"Wow!" she said shakily. "That was something."

He chuckled. "Do you always say whatever comes into your head?"

"Yes. Sometimes. Usually."

He laughed again as he threaded his fingers through her hair. "I like that. I like your openness. It's just another one of your exceptional attributes."

"Thank you, Will." She gazed at him through a romantic haze, his kiss still tingling on her lips. "I wonder . . ."

"Wonder what?" He pushed a strand of hair away from her face.

"If you would like to go to a party with me," she said quickly before she had a chance to change her mind.

"A party?"

"Yes, my friend Judy's having some people over next week, no big deal, just a get-together with friends. It'll be a lot of fun. I thought maybe you'd like to go with me—"

He hadn't actually moved away, but his arms had loosened; he'd broken the contact. "I don't think so, Kasey. Not a party."

"It'll be late—at night, when you seem to be more comfortable."

She didn't miss the tenseness in his jaw, the darkening of his eyes. "I appreciate the invitation. Another time, maybe." His voice was coolly polite.

She moved away to her door. "Maybe," she repeated, fighting back her disappointment. The warmth, the excitement of his kiss, was forgotten in his refusal. She couldn't understand the change in him. "I guess I'd better go in," she said a little stiffly, turning her key in the lock. "Thanks for the walk home."

"Sure. Good night, Kasey."

5

INSIDE HER APARTMENT, Kasey turned on the light and leaned against the door, wondering what had happened. Will hadn't faked the kiss or the emotions behind it; she was certain of that. Then why, so suddenly, had he acted like another person, cool and distant?

Kasey walked slowly down the hall, giving no thought to her surroundings, drifting toward the bedroom where she hit the switch on an art-deco lamp by the door and aimlessly dropped her handbag on a chair. Then she gazed at herself in the dressing-table mirror. She looked as perplexed as she felt.

Will definitely had an attitude. Why? Because she'd asked him to a party? Kasey dismissed that possibility as absurd. It was all too weird. And this wasn't the first time he'd reached out to her and then pulled away with no explanation. He didn't seem like someone who would play mind games, but that's how it looked. What the hell was the matter with the guy?

Kasey sank onto her bed. One thing was for sure. She wasn't going to share this story with Judy. Her friend had told her she was far too impetuous; this time, Judy was right.

WILL SAT in the middle of the sofa in the dark, staring out the balcony doors into the night beyond. He'd wanted to make things better with Kasey; he'd succeeded in making them worse.

More than an impulse had taken him to the restaurant tonight. He'd been possessed by a need to see her. And the kiss? It had seemed so natural, so right, and once he'd leaned toward her, touching her lips with his, he hadn't been able to hold back.

And why not? She was damned appealing, and she didn't even know it, which made her even more desirable. Her kiss had been an aphrodisiac, making him want more. He wondered what it would be like making love to her. Will shook his head slowly. He knew damned well what it would be like; it would be wonderful. He didn't dare let his mind go any further with that. He had to be careful, and he knew it.

But Will was tired of walking a tightrope. He'd survived his close call with the media. Careful scrutiny of the news footage had revealed that he'd been visible for only a few seconds and, with the beard, was virtually unrecognizable.

He'd taken a chance, with no harm done, so why not go to the party with her? A smile curved his lips. After all, as Kasey had said, it was at night—his time. And he wouldn't know anyone there.

Before he could change his mind, Will picked up the phone and called Information. She was listed. He punched in the number and waited through half a dozen rings for her to pick up.

"Kasey. This is Will. About that party..."

"Yes?" She sounded hesitant, cautious. He didn't blame her.

"You took me by surprise. Parties really aren't my thing recently, but you sounded like you really wanted to go."

"Yes." She seemed unsure of how to respond.

He was making her nervous, and Will didn't like that. He jumped right in. "Well, I'd like to go with you. In fact, I can't think of anything I'd rather do."

He heard her quick intake of breath and then the surprise in her voice. "Are you sure?"

"Very sure."

"Sometimes, I—" She hesitated. "Sometimes, I think you're playing games with me."

"This isn't a game. I want to go with you. Just tell me when."

"I will. As soon as I know, myself," she said with a relaxed laugh.

"Good." He waited a few seconds before adding, "Thanks for tonight. I enjoyed walking you at least part of the way home."

She laughed again, musically. "So did I. Thanks."

"My pleasure, and I mean it. I'll look forward to hearing from you about the party."

He clicked off the phone and stared into the dark. Kasey wasn't the only one with fantasies. Will was beginning to have a few of his own.

KASEY PUSHED through the crowd toward Judy and shouted in her friend's ear, "What a great party. I had no idea there would be so many people, or so many paintings!"

Judy grabbed Kasey's hand and pulled her across the huge art-filled Soho loft, past oil paintings that were framed and hanging, displayed on easels or stacked along the wall.

They ducked into a galley kitchen at the far end of the loft, and Judy closed the door. "I didn't hear a word you said."

"I said it's a great party," Kasey repeated a little less loudly. "Lots of paintings. Lots of people."

"Oh. That's better. Somewhat. Sound travels in this place, but at least it's big enough to put some distance between the music and the conversation. About the paintings—"

"They're great. Very—unusual. Dozens of pictures of the same scene!"

"Let's say Danny's into repetition. Right now, he's into still lifes of peppers and garlic and tomatoes. But you never know what'll happen when he picks up his brush," Judy said fondly. "He's really good, Kasey. A couple of galleries are showing him already. He makes me so proud."

"I don't blame you," Kasey said.

"Now, about the people. Many of them, the single-male variety, anyway, were invited with you in mind. Remember my plan?"

"Judy, you and Danny were due for a party. You didn't need me as an excuse."

Judy stood on tiptoe, rummaged through an upper cabinet, found a big bowl and pulled it down. "This should be good for the extra chips and salsa. They're going like crazy." She turned to Kasey. "'Course we didn't need an excuse. Danny loves to show off his place, not to mention his paintings, but the idea was for you to get out on your own—away from the guy who's running away from his wife—"

"Judy!"

"Sorry. The idea was to give you a big field to choose from, but you brought your own choice with you."

"I sure did," Kasey said, nibbling on the chips as Judy poured them into the bowl. "And I bought a new dress just for the occasion." Kasey did a half turn and struck a pose, showing off her short, formfitting slip dress.

"Love it, but you never wear black."

"I'm trying to look more sophisticated," Kasey replied. "Do you like the silver glitter?" She turned again.

"I like it, I like it," Judy said. "But I'm not the one who counts. Obviously you're wearing it for Will."

"Whom you *don't* like," Kasey said, putting her hands on her hips and confronting her friend with the statement.

"Says who?"

"You do. Talking about all the other men here—when he's the man I'm with."

"He's a good dancer," Judy said.

"Well, that's positive," Kasey replied sarcastically.

"It's true. Look at 'em. All but lining up to dance with him."

"How about you?" Kasey asked.

"Sure. I had my turn." Judy opened the refrigerator and replenished a tray of fresh vegetables.

"So? What do you think?"

"I told you," Judy equivocated. "He's a good dancer."

"What else?"

Judy closed the fridge with her hip. "Good-looking. I'd like to see him without a beard."

"Me, too," Kasey replied. "Sometimes I have a fantasy—" She broke off, under Judy's steady gaze. "Never mind. Go on."

"Well, he has fabulous clothes. And he brought the best wine—"

"Three bottles," Kasey reminded her, swiping a celery stick from the platter.

"But I don't know a damned thing about him. I asked a million questions and didn't find out a thing."

"So he doesn't like being interrogated. Who does?" Kasey had a sudden thought. "Oh, no. You didn't ask about his ex-wife, did you?"

"Please, give me some credit. I was very cool and casual, but he was, well, tricky. He answered but he didn't answer."

Kasey settled on a kitchen stool. "Explain."

"He was happy to talk about Bartow Tower and how he met you and how hot it is in the city in August and how he wishes he could get away. Why can't he get away? He doesn't have a job! My question is, what does he do all day?"

"You asked him that?" Kasey hoped for a negative answer.

"Not in so many words, but he knew damned well that was my implied question."

Kasey sighed silently. "I expect he's on a strict budget and doesn't go out very often because he can't afford to."

"Oh, sure. That's why he dresses like something out of *GQ* magazine and spends sixty or seventy dollars on wine for a crowd that's happy to drink out of five-dollar gallon jugs. No, Kasey, money isn't the guy's problem. Something's going on."

The door opened and Will stood there, looking quizzically at them.

Kasey held her breath for a moment, wondering if he'd been listening. When he smiled wryly and leaned against the doorjamb, she figured they were safe.

"Am I interrupting?" he asked.

"Nope," Judy said. "I'm just getting some food together to feed those animals out there." She picked up the bowl and platter.

"Actually, the animals sent me after the food," Will told her. "Let me help."

"It's okay. I'm ferrying out salsa, chips and veggies. This'll hold them for a while. Then it's Danny's turn. It's his party, too," she said as she scurried out.

"Not one of my big fans," Will commented.

"Untrue," Kasey defended. "Judy's busy with the party."

Will crossed the kitchen in two steps and stopped by the stool where Kasey sat. He put his hands lightly on her shoulders. "Doesn't matter. Just so you're on my side."

The touch of his hands on her bare skin was so pleasurable that it sent a ripple of heat flowing along her arms and shoulders.

"Have I told you what a knockout dress that is?"

Kasey felt herself glow at his words. "You did, but you can tell me again."

Will broke into laughter. "You're a rare find, Kasey, totally honest and unpretentious."

"I'm not sure I like being 'a find,'" she teased. "Sounds like something you stumble on in the street."

"Okay. How about rare treasure?" He leaned closer so that his face was against hers. He let his lips graze her face, his beard rub against her cheek. Then he turned slightly, his lips just a millimeter from her mouth. Kasey closed her eyes and slipped her arms around his waist, thinking that everything about the night was working out perfectly.

Then Danny burst into the kitchen and started rummaging in the refrigerator. He pulled out a hunk of cheese, put it on the counter and looked over at them, grinning. His sandy hair flopped in his face, which was flushed from dancing.

"Sorry, folks, but I've been sent on a cheese run."

"That's okay," Will responded as he lifted Kasey lightly from the stool and set her on her feet. "We were just going out to dance."

"There's a bunch of real hot CDs piled up out there," Danny told them. "Put one of them on, turn down the lights and tell Judy I'll be looking for her. You're not the only couple with romance on your minds," he added as he found more cheese, pulled off a chunk and with a grin popped it into his mouth.

WILL WORE a smoky-colored silk shirt. Her cheek rested against it. Her arms were clasped around his neck; his were locked around her waist. They'd given up any pretense of dancing and were standing in one spot, holding each other, swaying gently.

Kasey felt the cool fabric of his soft silky shirt and every muscle of his warm hard body pressed against her. All kinds of fantasies skipped in and out of her mind as Will kissed her tenderly, causing tremors in all her secret places. She had an urge to peel off his luxurious shirt and unzip his pleated linen trousers. She remembered that glimpse of him wearing only a towel, his skin gleaming with droplets of water, and the image caused her heart to beat faster. She closed her eyes tightly and imagined that she was wrapped in the towel with him and then immediately wondered what he would think of her X-rated fantasy.

Kasey knew what *she* thought. She recognized the symptoms. She was falling in love, and she was powerless to stop it. Despite Judy's warnings, despite all of her own questions about Will, she had been increasingly drawn to him. The more she'd seen of Will, the more she'd wanted to be with him.

She was involved, and there was nothing she could do about it now. She was falling, head over heels, for the man next door, the most exciting, handsome and mysterious man she'd ever met.

Will had let his hand drift up the bare skin of her back. She looked at him through a romantic haze as the conversation hummed, laughter rippled and music floated around them.

He looked deeply into her eyes and whispered, "A million dollars . . ."

"What? I don't—"

"Forget a penny. Your thoughts are worth a million dollars."

Kasey smiled widely. "I was thinking about how much fun I'm having with you, how much I like you. Thanks for coming to the party with me."

Will pulled her close with a sound she couldn't quite interpret. "Oh, Kasey, you don't know what you do to me when you look up with those angel-blue eyes and thank me. I should be thanking you for getting me out of that damned apartment."

Kasey snuggled contentedly against him. She had no desire to do what she'd done before—ask questions about Will's life-style, his tendency to hole up in his apartment, to rarely venture out in the light of day. It was his business, not hers. She was content with Will as she knew him, without interrogation. This was her night of nights and she was falling in love.

THEY LEFT the party late but still far ahead of the crowd, decided to take the subway uptown and walked leisurely through Soho to the station, arm in arm. Kasey felt relaxed and happy. The sky was clear and filled with stars and a slight breeze stirred the trees along Bleeker Street.

They paused to window-shop at bookstores, art galleries and funky boutiques, where Will kept Kasey amused by choosing outfits and fantasizing her dressed in them.

"There," he said at one of the more outrageous shops. "The long skirt with that crazy pattern. It's kind of slinky and hugs your figure just right." He looked her up and down. "The suede shoes, see them? Look at those heels. They're like stilts. You're wobbling a little."

Kasey held on to his arm, giggling at the scenario.

"Now, what about exposing some skin in that skimpy halter with that brown stuff hanging from it?"

By now, Kasey was laughing outright. "That 'brown stuff' is called fringe, and I sort of like that halter."

"I'd get it for you but unfortunately the shop's closed," Will said with a grin followed by a big hug as they moved on, occasionally dodging pedestrians who walked four abreast, turning the streets into their own giant party.

The subway station was nearly deserted when they went down the steps. Will bought two tokens at the booth, and they pushed through the turnstiles.

"No one here," he observed. "Which probably means we just missed a train and have a long wait."

"I don't mind," Kasey said, aware that she didn't. With Will beside her, even hanging out in an empty subway station sounded like fun. "We can check out the Broadway-show posters."

"Or decipher the graffiti. Let's see. What do you think this says?" He stopped before neon scribbling. "Whoops. I think I translated it. You better look the other way, Kasey."

"Is it pornographic?"

"Yep. Says, 'Kilroy was here.'"

"You're kidding! Kasey examined the lettering. "Isn't it crazy how everything comes back into vogue, even dumb slogans?"

"Like 'I can't believe I ate the whole thing,'" Will offered, quoting the old television commercial.

"Speaking of believing, how about 'Would you believe . . . ?'" Kasey giggled. "Wasn't that from 'Get Smart'?"

"Yes, and it's 'verrry interesting,'" Will offered, joining in her laughter.

"'But stupid!'" Laughing harder, Kasey held up her hand. "No more," she said, "or you'll have to carry me to the train."

"Sounds like a good idea. 'Go ahead, make my day!'" he said in a perfect Clint Eastwood imitation. He bent over to pick her up, when a thundering noise came down the stairs toward them. A crowd of young people, wildly dressed, some wearing masks, pushed through the turnstiles and poured onto the platform.

"Looks like someone opened the doors at a costume party and let 'em all out," Will observed.

"Or they're refugees from a screening of *The Rocky Horror Picture Show*," Kasey decided.

"This is great," Will said as they were surrounded by the crowd. He leaned close to Kasey and whispered, "Though I'll never get used to women with purple crew cuts."

"Check out her friend, the guy with the tie-dyed hair," Kasey answered. Orange, green and blue." She gave a playful shudder. "But it's the nose rings that get me. That must hurt."

"Look at the woman over there—near the guy in the white makeup—she has a ring in her belly button."

Kasey laughed. "Of course, you'd notice that."

"I'm not really into rings in odd places. Besides, I only have eyes for you, Kasey," he said, grabbing her hand. "Let's walk down to the end of the platform."

Their hands touched for a moment before they were separated by the crowd. "I'm behind you," Kasey called out.

Then, before she could catch up with him, she found herself at the edge of the platform. She saw Will look back toward her. Then she couldn't see him at all and hoped he'd backtracked and would come around behind her.

Kasey heard the sound of the train in the distance and saw the yellow light far down the tunnel. She pushed her way back from the edge and saw Will coming toward her. Reaching out, she could almost touch him.

The roar of the train grew louder, and Kasey turned to look down the tracks as the train approached. She could feel the platform shake and vibrate. As she tried to move away, she felt a push and was suddenly teetering on the edge of the platform.

Fighting for balance, Kasey flailed her arms, trying desperately to push away from the edge as the train, an iron and steel monster, rushed toward the station.

Her mouth was open. She was screaming. But the scream was silent, caught deep inside. And Kasey seemed to be looking at the scene from outside herself, watching as an arm pushed her, watching as she struggled to scream.

Then she closed her eyes and gave up. She was going to fall. She was going to die.

A strong hand reached out, grabbed her arm and pulled her away as the train sped into the station.

"My God, Kasey, what the hell—" Will's arms were tight around her, and she clung to him, digging her nails into his back through the softness of his shirt.

"Will, oh, Will," she cried. "Someone pushed me. I felt it, saw it—" Her knees trembled and her body began to shake, sending her into convulsions as all around, people surged and pushed their way onto the train. No one else seemed to have noticed her near-death experience.

"Let's get out of here," Will shouted over the din. "We'll find a taxi."

"No! I want to get on the train and go home—now!" she cried as she pushed and pulled her way through the crowd just as the doors started to close.

Will blocked the entrance, his back to the sliding door, holding it open while Kasey squeezed through.

The car was packed, and they stood up, with Kasey holding on to the center pole while Will wrapped his arms around her from behind, his hands enclosing hers on the pole. Kasey could feel the tears streaming down her face.

At Times Square, the throng cleared out and Will led her to a seat. His face was grave and attentive, and he didn't let go of her hand.

"Why would someone try to kill me?" Kasey asked, looking at Will.

"No one was trying to kill you, Kasey," he said, brushing at her tears with his hand. "There was a huge crowd, people jockeying for position—"

"You're wrong," she cried out.

He held her tightly. "It's all right, Kasey. You're upset, and there's good reason. Someone bumped into you, and you almost fell onto the tracks."

"I was pushed," Kasey insisted. "I felt someone push me. I saw hands, arms. A man. A woman. I don't know." She buried her face against him.

Will held her silently as the train pulled out of the station.

Neither of them spoke again until they reached the Seventy-second Street stop. "Here we are," he said, helping her up.

"Thanks. I'm sorry I was so . . ."

"Don't be sorry. It was frightening for you." They left the train and walked toward the exit.

"Yes. I could have died. If it hadn't been for . . ." She stopped and looked up at him. "If it hadn't been for you! Will, you saved me. You grabbed me and pulled me back from certain death. Oh, Will, thank you. Thank you." Her fingers clutched desperately at his sleeve.

He put his arm around her and led her up the stairs to the street. "We'll be home soon, Kasey. Then you'll be safe. Nothing will happen to you. I swear."

WILL TOOK Kasey's key from her hand and opened the door. "I'll come in with you if you don't mind, just for a moment."

"For a little longer, if *you* don't mind," she said. "I don't want to be alone."

"I'll stay as long as you'll let me stay," he replied with a smile.

Kasey turned on the light and led Will down the hall to her living room, flipping on more lights as she crossed the room, comforted by the familiarity of her apartment.

"Would you like something to drink? Coffee—or wine? I think I have a bottle over here." She moved toward a black lacquered cabinet in the corner of the room. Adrenaline still pumped through her body. She couldn't forget the terror of teetering on the edge of the platform. And she couldn't ignore the excitement of having Will in her apartment.

"Nothing to drink," he replied, glancing around the apartment. "The place looks like you. Bright and modern. Makes a statement and stands by it. Sound familiar?"

"Thanks for the compliment, but right now all that matters is that I'm here and not on the subway tracks—" She felt a tremor in her voice and was afraid she would break down again, when he caught hold of her hand.

"Come and sit by me. It's time to relax." He settled her on the sofa and sat down beside her.

"I can't forget that you saved my life, Will."

He put a finger across her lips. "It's over, Kasey. Don't think about it now."

"I can't help it, I—"

"Think of something pleasant," he insisted. "Think of the fun you had at the party." He smiled slyly, adding, "Dancing with me, of course."

She returned his smile, and as she remembered being in his arms, he held her close. She blocked the subway incident from her mind and filled her thoughts with Will. She wanted him to stay here with her, holding her, not just for a few minutes, but for the rest of the night.

"Are you thinking good thoughts?" he asked softly.

"Yes." Suddenly, she shivered involuntarily, reminded of the incident.

"Sorry," she whispered.

"You're thinking about it, aren't you?"

She nodded.

"It's all right. It's normal. We just have to get you totally relaxed. Lean forward," he ordered in a gentle voice, "and I'll massage your neck. I bet your muscles are as tight as piano wires."

Obediently, Kasey dropped her head and felt Will's thumbs at the base of her neck. He moved them in a firm, circular motion that sent tremors racing along her nerve endings.

"I was right," he murmured. "Your muscles are in knots, but I can take care of that."

The pressure of his fingers and thumbs increased, and the tension began to flow from her. Safe beside him, the memory of what had happened started to fade.

"Better?"

"Yes, much."

As he moved his hands over her upper body, Kasey's skin grew warm and pliant, and slowly the heat of his touch melted through the tenseness of her muscles. The delightful warmth spread along her neck, across her shoulders, down her back. Everywhere that he touched her. She let out a deep sigh of contentment. The scene at the subway blurred some more, then disappeared.

"Mmm," she said with a moan, rolling her head in a lazy circle. "Don't stop. This is wonderful."

She leaned back against him, amazed that she'd ever been wary of him. His sense of authority, the coiled power beneath his smooth image and the whisper of arrogance in his voice were all things that had made him seem dangerous. Now, those were the very things that gave her a deep sense of security. High in Bartow Tower, with the rest of the world far, far away, she felt completely safe.

His fingers touched a tight spot on her shoulder, pressed and massaged until the tightness vanished. She made little mewing sounds of pleasure at the release of tension. "Oh, oh, oh." She sighed. "Mmm. That feels so good."

He leaned close, his breath warm against her neck. "I'm crazy about the sound effects."

She flushed and turned to look at him. "Sorry, I got carried away."

"Don't say you're sorry, not ever. I want you to be carried away. Oh, how I want that."

He took her face in his hands, devouring her with his eyes. His gentle, practiced thumbs made tiny circles on her temples. Kasey was caught up in his eyes, drawn into their dark depths. Her heart started beating erratically as a delicious warmth shimmered over her skin. She took a deep breath and closed her eyes, melting into his arms.

Will bent forward and kissed her, giving himself over to the feeling of her mouth against his. What was it about her that made him forget all the rules he'd set up? She gave another of those delicious little moans and moved toward him, and Will understood exactly what it was. It was her candor. Her eager response to his touch. The way she returned his kisses.

He pulled her across his lap and felt her softness against him, felt the need and desire in her body that mirrored his own. He traced the soft skin of her leg with his fingers, along her smooth calf, across her knee, under her short skirt. His hands moved as if on their own, hungrily, almost desperately, over her body.

The blood pounded wildly in Will's head, and desire flowed through him hot and hard. Being with Kasey was like a tug-of-war, a battle to maintain control. A battle he was losing.

In his arms, Kasey was washed by a wave of dizzying pleasure. As his mouth captured hers, firm and demanding, the sensations became too powerful to resist. Kasey knew she was at the edge of something wonderful—and dangerous. The danger came from her feelings for Will, feelings so intense, she knew acting on them would change her life forever.

"I want you, Will," she whispered. She couldn't stop the words any more than she could stop her feelings. Life was so precious; she wanted to reach out for it. Greedily. Hungrily.

"My Kasey," he murmured. "So open and honest. I love that about you."

She pulled at the buttons of his shirt and fumbled with his belt and zipper.

"And I love your actions as much as your words." He sought her lips again.

Their kiss deepened and they tasted each other hungrily. She felt his hardness through the fabric of his linen pants, and she wanted to touch him, really touch him, needing to feel his flesh beneath her fingers.

She unzipped him and touched him there, where she'd ached to caress him. She heard his gasp of pleasure.

He looked down at her, his eyes dark with passion; his voice was hoarse. "I want to touch you, too, Kasey. I want to undress you and make love to you, and—"

Kasey's kiss stopped his words, and as he kissed her back, he fumbled with her dress, which was nothing but an encumbrance, and she pushed away his silk shirt. Frantically, breaths coming in short gasps, they pulled off their clothes, leaving a tangle of lace and silk forgotten on the floor.

Her hands were insistent and seeking across his chest. She kissed him, inhaled his heat, tasted the saltiness of his skin. Her lips sought his flat brown nipples, her hands splayed across his back. She put her face against his chest and pressed closer to him. She wanted to become one with him, to merge with him. She wanted her breath to be his breath, his heartbeat hers. Her pulse beat urgently, as out of control as Kasey herself.

And she didn't care.

They were on the floor now, Will bending over her, licking her neck, kissing her chin, brushing her lips with his, tasting, releasing, tasting again.

His gasps of pleasure fanned the flames of her need, and she shifted so that she could touch the hard shaft of his manhood, and feel him grow beneath her fingers.

"You're driving me crazy," he cried.

"Then make love to me, Will," she answered. "I can't wait another second." Could that possibly be her voice, Kasey wondered. It seemed so far away, so desperate with desire. Yes! It *was* her voice, begging him for the intimacy that would make them one, frantic to be joined with him when she sought closeness as never before in her life.

"We won't wait, Kasey," he whispered in a voice heavy with desire.

She guided him into her warmth, arching her back, straining to meet him. He filled her inch by inch until she thought she would scream with pleasure. They moved together in a kind of primitive rhythm, with no hesitation, no holding back, a ritual of desire that brought Kasey to the edge of ecstasy.

She dug her fingers into the smooth muscles of his back, wrapped her legs around him, moved with him and breathed with him. Their eyes met and locked. Every part of her melted into him, and as the exquisite pressure within her built, grew, twisted and threatened to explode, he thrust deeper and deeper, taking her to the brink of something wonderful.

Then the moment of highest pleasure was upon them, and they held on to it as long as they could until it exploded for them in shimmering waves of passion.

Will wrapped his arms around her and held her tightly. She could feel the thudding of his heart, as wild and out of control as her own. She listened as both heartbeats began to slow a little and finally near a normal level as he kissed her forehead and pushed her damp hair away from her face. "Next time, I'll take my time and love every inch of you," he said softly.

She pressed against him, wishing she could become a part of him. But the next best thing was simply to lie next to him, her body touching his, bathed in the afterglow of love.

"It was perfect," she whispered. "Perfect." She didn't add that he was her fantasy come true.

He chuckled low in his throat. "We can improve, even on perfection, Kasey. And we have all night to do it."

6

WITHOUT OPENING her eyes, Kasey rolled over in bed and moved her hand along the rumpled sheet beside her. Empty. Then she remembered. She and Will had slept in each other's arms, wakened at dawn and made slow, languorous love as the sun rose over the city. Then he had kissed her lightly, promised to see her later, given her bottom a pat and told her to go back to sleep.

She'd taken that advice and then some, Kasey realized as she finally opened her eyes and looked at the clock.

"It can't be ten o'clock," she said out loud. But it was. She'd slept like a baby. No wonder, Kasey thought as she gave a sigh of satisfaction and snuggled against her pillow. Last night had been the most intense experience of her life. In a few short hours, she'd felt the chill of fear and tasted the sweetness of joy.

Kasey truly believed that she'd faced death in the subway station, but she had never felt more alive than when Will had made love to her. Spine-tingling, earth-moving, heaven-shaking love. She stretched voluptuously and let her mind dwell on each episode in his arms. After the almost frantic lovemaking on the floor of her living room, he'd carried her to bed where they'd taken their time exploring, getting to know each other's bodies before making love again. They'd slept for a while, awakened before dawn and surprised themselves with the renewal of their passion. And then, before Will left . . .

"That's four times!" Kasey said as she sat up in bed. Never had she even imagined such sexual saturation, and judging by the feelings that were coming over her now, if Will were anywhere near, she would have done her best to seduce him back to bed. She was obsessed; no doubt about it. With the mysterious man next door. With a stranger. Well, not quite a stranger. She smiled slyly.

It sounded crazy, but in fact it was wonderful, Kasey thought as she closed her eyes and fell back on the pillow. So what if she'd known Will for barely ten days. So what if she'd dated him once—twice, if she counted the picnic. What did time matter when they were so perfect together, when he made her feel so free? Last night, time certainly hadn't mattered; nothing had mattered except being with him.

She hadn't thought about why it was happening. She'd just given herself over to her fantasy, experiencing with her senses, not her mind. And what she'd experienced was joy, pleasure and wonder.

If she was crazy, then hats off to craziness, Kasey decided, pushing away dark thoughts as she gave in to the memory of kissing Will, touching him . . .

The jarring sound of the doorbell roused Kasey from her daydreams. She hit the floor running, pulling on her robe as she headed down the hall. Will had decided to come back for coffee, she imagined. To bring her a pastry. Maybe breakfast in bed. She threw open the door. And tried to hide her disappointment when she saw Glenna standing there.

Her neighbor was dressed in her work uniform, as Glenna called it: suit, blouse and jogging shoes for the walk to her office.

"You didn't ask who was at the door, Kasey," Glenna chastised. "That's dangerous."

"I know. I was thinking—well, about something else." She smiled at Glenna. "Come on in. Coffee?"

Glenna stepped inside, closed the door and followed Kasey down the hall. "Don't have time. Unless you have that vanilla-flavored—"

"All out," Kasey told her.

"Oh. Then I don't really have time," Glenna said with a laugh. "So I guess I'd better ask my favor. Lo Mein, this weekend?" Glenna ducked her head.

"Don't look so sheepish," Kasey said. "I'll take care of the cat." She poured herself some coffee and looked at Glenna questioningly.

"Okay. Just half a cup." Glenna leaned against the doorjamb, watching Kasey. "You look—different," she said.

Kasey tried not to react. "What do you mean?"

"I'm not sure. Just a feeling. Did you know that I met our sexy new neighbor?"

The sudden change in conversation startled Kasey. Already caught off-balance, she forced herself to concentrate on pouring the coffee.

"He's nothing like Count Dracula, by the way," Glenna went on. "He's about as hunky as they come. He came over to my apartment," she added, raising her dark eyebrows suggestively.

Kasey stopped in midmotion. "Oh?" She was stunned at the stab of jealousy she felt, sharp and primeval.

"Yep, he returned Lo Mein one night. You know how he crosses from balcony to balcony? The cat, not the hunk," she added with a smile. "Anyway, you were right about one thing. He's *sooo* good-looking and—"

"And?" Kasey managed to ask.

"Totally impervious to my charms."

Kasey let out the breath she'd been holding. "What happened?"

"I asked him in and he declined." She formed her bright red lips into a pout. "Have you had any better luck?"

Kasey hesitated. She didn't want to lie, and yet she wanted to keep her relationship with Will personal and private. Something special. She compromised. "I've seen him a time or two."

Glenna looked surprised. "Really? Well, a little summer fling with the man next door . . ."

"I didn't say that," Kasey objected.

"You didn't have to. I see the blush." Glenna narrowed her eyes and peered at Kasey more closely. "Or is that whisker burn on your cheeks?"

Kasey couldn't keep her hand from flying to her face.

"So, I'm right," Glenna said. "And green with envy."

Kasey realized with surprise and concern that Glenna's voice echoed her words. She *was* jealous! Kasey looked away and said nothing.

"Well, I'd like to hear all about it," Glenna said, glancing at her watch. "But I'm late, so—" She walked toward the door, adding over her shoulder, "Thanks for taking care of Lo Mein. Again."

As Kasey watched Glenna leave, she found herself thinking about her neighbor's comments. She'd referred to a "little summer fling with the man next door." Probably that's what others would assume, too, that Kasey was an impetuous fool, acting out a fantasy with a mysterious stranger.

She leaned against the kitchen counter and sipped her coffee. Okay, she'd admit to the fantasy of making love to a stranger; she'd even plead temporary insanity brought on by an excess of passion, but she wasn't going to dismiss the way she felt about Will. He made her laugh, and he made her *feel* as never before.

She was falling in love!

Then she stopped her fantasizing and scolded herself aloud. "You've got it bad, Kasey. Slow down. Take your time."

But she didn't want to slow down. She wanted the hours to fly by until the night—when she would see Will again.

The ringing of the phone interrupted her reverie, and she picked up the receiver abstractedly.

"Hello," she said, suddenly thinking the call might be from Will.

There was no response.

"Hello," she repeated. Again, no reply, but Kasey was sure she could hear someone on the line, listening, waiting.

"Hello. Who is this?" Her voice became sharper.

The line went dead.

Kasey frowned and hung up. Someone with a wrong number and no manners, she decided. She poured another cup of coffee and headed to the bedroom. The phone rang again.

Once more, when she answered, there was the eerie silence on the other end. But this time, she was sure she heard slow, steady breathing. It must be someone playing a game, she told herself, a sick game that she wasn't in the mood to play.

She hung up, turned on her answering machine and headed for the shower.

Later, before she left for an early staff meeting at Windows, she checked her messages, hoping for one from Will. Instead, she heard three more hang-ups. And now, they did more than irritate her; they frightened her. She felt the hair along the back of her neck prickle as she listened to the breathing. It was ominous and threatening.

Then she realized, suddenly and clearly, what was happening. Carl Dandridge was harassing her again! It had to be Carl. It was just like him to use a sneaky, irritating method like anonymous phone calls to get to her.

Once Kasey figured that out, the fear passed and she became angry. She wasn't going to take it. If he didn't tire very quickly of this little game, she'd simply change her number. She wouldn't let his childish tricks ruin her day. It was a day when she wanted to do nothing more than bask in the memory of her night with Will.

And think about the night to come.

BY EIGHT O'CLOCK that evening, Kasey's mood was as dark as the storm clouds that had rolled in over the city. Rain fell in sheets, and lightning flashed in jagged lines, illuminating the city's skyline. Inside Walk-by-Windows, clouds of equal darkness hung over Chef Albert's kitchen.

Albert stood in the middle of the large room pointing a big wooden spoon at Kasey. "'Ow could you do this to me, Kasey?"

"Do what, Albert? I don't know what you're talking about."

"Pleeze to look." He aimed the spoon away from Kasey and toward the counter. "All of theese lobsters. Always, I make the order, and the last time, you tell me I order too much of the lobster. Is not true?" His face was turning red.

"Yes, it's true."

"But I use them all, is not true?" He pointed the spoon back at Kasey.

She nodded. "I didn't realize you were perfecting your new dish, Albert. You went over my budget, but it worked out, I believe. We'll get a good review from Mattison Monroe. That will more than make up for the cost of the extra lobster."

"But what 'appens about the extra cost of theese lobsters. You worry about cost, then why do you go over my head and bring to me three times the lobster as I need? Why you do thees to me, Kasey?"

"I do not do thees to you, Albert," she said, and then caught herself. "I mean, you're the one with the tendency to overorder. Not me."

He didn't appear to be listening. "Even if we get the good review and everyone come to have my Lobster Albert, theese are too many." As his face got redder, his voice got louder.

"Albert, listen to me. I didn't—"

"And it 'appens at dinnertime when I am over my elbows in orders. Where to put so much of lobster? What to do?"

"I don't know, Albert, but I *didn't* place the order," she said quickly before he could interrupt again.

"Then 'ow it shows up 'ere, eh, if I do not make and you do not make? Thees is what I wish to know." His face was beet red now. "You are in charge, or so I believe. Look what you do to me. *Mon Dieu*, 'ow can I use all theese lobsters?"

"I'm sure we can think of something, Albert." Kasey kept her voice low, hoping to bring Albert's thundering down to her level. The last thing she wanted was for patrons seated near the kitchen to hear the chef's tirade.

"Is impossible to keep them all alive. I 'ave not enough tanks."

"Fill up some pots and pans with water and dump the lobsters in them."

"How can I do thees?" Albert shook his head in disbelief that Kasey would suggest such a thing. "Each pot, each pan, I need for my cooking. Theese lobsters, they will be crawling out of the tank while I am try to cook dinner for sixty patrons, and with only one sous chef." He looked around to see the young man at the stove, in white pants, shirt, apron and hat, staring with open mouth.

"See? He stops to look. Cook, cook!" he ordered.

The sous-chef closed his mouth and began to furiously stir a sauce on the stove.

Soon, theese lobsters, they will be walking out zee door into zee restaurant," Albert said.

"We'll stop short of a lobster rebellion, Albert. That I promise."

"Hmmph," he said.

"I'll call the wholesaler right away and find out what's going on. Maybe I can convince him to take some of the lobster back."

"Thees is good," he said. "But you understand, I must tell Fred about all that is 'appen."

"I understand. In fact, I'll tell Fred myself." Kasey grimaced when she thought about the manager's reaction and the extra cost to the restaurant. "The point is, I didn't order all the lobster, Albert. I didn't order *any* of it. But now we're crawling with lobster, to use an unfortunate term," she said, waiting for Albert to pick up on that theme.

"Yes, and soon they crawl—"

"I know. Out of the kitchen into the patrons' laps."

"So who 'as done thees to you, *ma petite?* Who wishes to cause you so much of problems?"

"Good question, Albert, and I think I know the answer."

JUDY STUCK her head into the kitchen. "Kasey, can I talk to you? We have a problem."

Kasey groaned aloud and headed for the door as one of the lobsters crawled out of its packing box and dropped to the floor in front of her. She looked at Al-

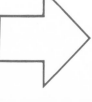

NO COST! NO OBLIGATION TO BUY!
NO PURCHASE NECESSARY!

PLAY "LUCKY 7" AND GET FIVE FREE GIFTS!

HOW TO PLAY:

1. With a coin, carefully scratch off the silver box at the right. Then check the claim chart to see what we have for you—FREE BOOKS and a gift—ALL YOURS! ALL FREE!

2. Send back this card and you'll receive brand-new Harlequin Temptation® novels. These books have a cover price of $3.25 each, but they are yours to keep absolutely free.

3. There's no catch. You're under no obligation to buy anything. We charge nothing—ZERO—for your first shipment. And you don't have to make any minimum number of purchases—not even one!

4. The fact is thousands of readers enjoy receiving books by mail from the Harlequin Reader Service®. They like the convenience of home delivery...they like getting the best new novels before they're available in stores...and they love our discount prices!

5. We hope that after receiving your free books you'll want to remain a subscriber. But the choice is yours—to continue or cancel, anytime at all! So why not take us up on our invitation, with no risk of any kind. You'll be glad you did!

You'll love this plush, cuddly Teddy Bear, an adorable accessory for your dressing table, bookcase or desk. Measuring 5½" tall, he's soft and brown and has a bright red ribbon around his neck—he's completely captivating! And he's yours *absolutely free*, when you accept this no-risk offer!

PLAY "LUCKY 7"

**Just scratch off the silver box with a coin.
Then check below to see the gifts you get.**

YES! I have scratched off the silver box. Please send me all the gifts for which I qualify. I understand I am under no obligation to purchase any books, as explained on the back and on the opposite page.

142 CIH AWLY
(U-H-T-09/95)

NAME

ADDRESS   APT.

CITY   STATE   ZIP

 WORTH FOUR FREE BOOKS PLUS A FREE CUDDLY TEDDY BEAR

 WORTH THREE FREE BOOKS

 WORTH TWO FREE BOOKS

 WORTH ONE FREE BOOK

DETACH AND MAIL CARD TODAY

THE HARLEQUIN READER SERVICE®: HERE'S HOW IT WORKS

Accepting free books places you under no obligation to buy anything. You may keep the books and gift and return the shipping statement marked "cancel". If you do not cancel, about a month later we'll send you 4 additional novels, and bill you just $2.66 each plus 25¢ delivery and applicable sales tax, if any.* That's the complete price, and—compared to cover prices of $3.25 each—quite a bargain! You may cancel at any time, but if you choose to continue, every month we'll send you 4 more books, which you may either purchase at the discount price...or return at our expense and cancel your subscription.

*Terms and prices subject to change without notice. Sales tax applicable in N.Y.

BUSINESS REPLY MAIL
FIRST CLASS MAIL   PERMIT NO. 717   BUFFALO, NY

POSTAGE WILL BE PAID BY ADDRESSEE

HARLEQUIN READER SERVICE
3010 WALDEN AVE
PO BOX 1867
BUFFALO NY 14240-9952

NO POSTAGE
NECESSARY
IF MAILED
IN THE
UNITED STATES

bert, who shrugged while the sous-chef rushed over, picked it up, nimbly avoiding the claws, smiled broadly at Kasey and tossed the lobster back in the box.

Albert's prediction was coming true very quickly, Kasey thought as she waited to hear the most recent bad news from Judy, who didn't seem to notice the lobster invasion.

"It's that reservation you took for the party of twelve. They haven't showed yet, and I have patrons waiting to be seated."

Kasey followed Judy into the dining room. "Let me make a call first, and I'll be right there," she said.

"Kasey—"

"This can't wait, Judy."

"Neither can—"

But Kasey was on her way to the phone. While Judy waited impatiently, she begged, implored and argued her way into a deal with the wholesaler. He finally agreed to take back at least half the lobster but only after he was convinced she hadn't placed the order.

When Kasey hung up, she had visions of cold lobster salad for days to come, but that was better than the lobster attack on the patrons anticipated by Albert.

"Okay," she said to Judy. "Next problem."

As they walked toward the reservations desk, Judy told her, "According to the log, your party of twelve was supposed to arrive at seven-thirty. It's after eight now. I had to rearrange section three to make room for this group. And they're still not here." She gestured toward the table. Twelve empty chairs in an otherwise packed restaurant.

Kasey nodded wordlessly.

"There're twice that many patrons waiting in the bar for their tables," Judy reminded her. "And I've turned away a whole slew of people without reservations. Angry people, who weren't that wild about going back out into the rain when they saw a dozen empty seats. Since you made the reservation, I thought—"

Kasey glanced at the book. "Yep, here it is, and I made it. Party of twelve. H. Johnson." She picked up the reservations phone, punched in the number, listened and then slammed down the receiver.

"What—"

"H. Johnson is the Howard Johnson Hotel."

"Kasey, what's going on?" Judy asked.

"I've been wondering about that most of the night. Since this afternoon, actually," she said, thinking of the hang-ups on her home phone. "I think I've figured it out. Carl Dandridge is behind all of this."

"He made the reservation?"

"Hear me out, Judy. First, he threatened me in person and then again when he talked to Fred. Today, he started harassing me. I got hang-ups every time the phone rang at my apartment this morning. Then I arrived at work only to find that an army of lobster had taken over the kitchen, ordered—supposedly—by me, the wholesaler said. Obviously, someone impersonating me. And now this, taking reservations for people who don't exist."

"Didn't you recognize his voice when he called?"

Kasey thought about that for a moment. "It wasn't Carl. A woman made the reservation, at his insistence, I'm sure, probably the same woman who impersonated me to order the lobster." She looked at Judy through narrowed eyes. "I've had it with this guy, Judy. This is going to stop."

"Uh-oh, that look makes me nervous. Are you planning to do something foolish?"

"I don't know whether it's foolish or not, but I'm going to do something. I'm going to confront the sneaky bastard and I'm going to do it tonight." She slammed down the reservations book and headed toward the office. "I'm getting his address and going to his apartment now."

"No, you aren't." Judy grabbed Kasey's arm. "That's insane. Wait—"

"I'm not waiting. I'm settling the problem once and for all."

"This could be dangerous," Judy said, lowering her voice. "I'll go back to the office with you and we can talk, maybe figure out—"

Kasey shook off her friend's hand and kept walking.

"Please, be sensible." Judy walked along beside Kasey. "Remember when you had the confrontation with Carl? It was scary, wasn't it?"

Kasey hesitated. "Well . . ."

"I know it was, and you weren't alone with him. You were in a restaurant full of people."

They reached the office, and Kasey replied honestly, "I actually *was* alone, way back here with no one close by. And I *was* a little frightened at first. But I knew I could handle him. Or at least I thought I could. I didn't really have to put myself to the test," she remembered, "because one of the busboys came by and scared him off."

"See? What do you think will happen when you come face-to-face with him, alone, in his apartment?"

"You're right," Kasey admitted.

"So you're not going?"

Kasey pushed open the office door. "I'm still going." She opened the file drawer and pulled out the employee records. "But I'm not going alone. You're going to lend me a protector, your most pumped-up waiter would be a good choice. That's probably Rinaldo, huh?

"Absolutely. Lifts weights, studies karate. A real specimen, our Rinaldo. Not much of a waiter, but what the hell? At a time like this, we discover his worth. I'll go round him up," Judy said.

"Great." Kasey pulled Carl's card from the file. "Tell him what's going on and ask him to hail a taxi."

After Judy left, Kasey wrote down Carl's address, put on her raincoat and gathered up the courage to confront Carl.

Judy was waiting at the front door.

"Did you send Rinaldo for a taxi?"

"Yes, but before you go—"

"No more advice, please. I can handle this problem."

"I'm sure. But there's another problem that's more immediate. There's a woman in the bar raising hell."

Kasey cursed under her breath.

"She says she's going to sue but no one can figure out why. She's ranting and raving—"

"Tell Rinaldo to hold the taxi. I'll be right out." Wondering what more could possibly go wrong, Kasey went into the bar.

Candles flickered romantically at the oak tables. The bartender wiped his already shining bar. Patrons waiting for their tables chatted quietly. In the sports corner, two men watched a ball game on television.

Kasey crossed to the bar. "Where is she, Mack?"

The bartender put down his cloth. "You mean the crazy redhead?"

"I guess. The one who was threatening to sue us."

Mack laughed. "Yeah. Said I watered her gin. I didn't but somebody should! She just walked out the side door, still going strong. Maybe you can catch her."

Kasey went to the door and looked out into the rainy night. A woman in a dark raincoat was getting into a cab. She didn't have an umbrella, and drops of rain shimmered in her brilliant bottle-red hair.

Deciding there wasn't time tonight for a confrontation, Kasey let the woman go and returned to the bar where Judy was waiting with Mack. "Do either of you know her?" she asked.

Judy shook her head.

"Never seen her before," Mack said. "Looks like a real strange dame. Kinda put together wrong, if you know what I mean."

"I don't have the slightest idea what you mean," Kasey said with a laugh. "But I'm not going to worry about her tonight. She didn't seem to bother anyone."

"Nope. 'Fact, it was a kinda interesting show. The guys watching the ball game even took it in for a couple of minutes."

"Well, let's hope it's the last show of the night."

"It might be if you stay put," Judy volunteered.

But Kasey was already heading for the front door. "Not a chance. Where's Rinaldo?"

"Waiting with the cab, just like you asked. But please be careful, Kasey. Don't do anything foolish."

"This isn't foolish," Kasey replied. "This is one of the smartest things I've done."

THE TAXI, slowed by the rain, crept north on Broadway, inch by inch. Horns blared pointlessly as drivers cursed each other, the city and the weather.

It didn't seem to bother Rinaldo, who took advantage of the available time to describe his physical prowess in the art of karate. If he were only half as skillful as he boasted, Kasey decided, she'd be in no danger from Carl. Or from anyone in the Western Hemisphere.

But Kasey didn't pay much attention to Rinaldo's bravado. She was lost in her own thoughts, mentally putting the pieces of the Carl Dandridge puzzle together. Most of them fitted. The bullying threats. The harassing phone calls. The stupid tricks to cause problems at the restaurant. All of that was vintage Carl, underhanded, devious and cowardly.

But the subway push? That was different. She could understand Carl's trying to make life miserable for her, but she couldn't imagine him trying to kill her. Besides, she hadn't seen Carl at the subway station and he wasn't the type to go out dancing, dressed up in costume, with a throng of party goers. Not Carl, not from what she knew of him and his contempt for the dance-club crowd.

She sat back with a sigh. Could he have followed her into the subway, mingled with the crowd, maybe even swiped someone's costume or mask—she wouldn't put *that* past him—and then decided to push her, not to kill her, but just to frighten her. That was more Carl's style. "The mealy little bastard," she said aloud.

"What is it, Kasey?"

"Nothing. Just thinking out loud about Carl, I guess."

"Cussing out loud is more like it. But that's okay, Kasey. I'm not one of those guys who thinks gals shouldn't talk tough."

"Oh, please, Rinaldo. Just saying that makes you one of those guys."

"No, really, Kasey—"

"Don't worry. Your attitude doesn't bother me, Rinaldo, as long as you can help me handle Carl."

The taxi stopped at a shabby brownstone near Columbia University, and Kasey asked the driver to wait. "We won't be very long."

Rinaldo rolled his shoulders and flexed his biceps as they climbed the steps to the apartment porch. "I'm ready, Kasey. I can take Carl. And it's gonna be a real pleasure."

"I'm glad you're confident," Kasey told him. "But remember that you're only here to show force, not to use it."

Kasey perused the tenant list at the front door. "I don't see his name." She rechecked the address she'd written down. "This is the right number, but there's no Carl Dandridge listed."

"How about this one, apartment four? There's no name by the buzzer."

"You're right. Let's try it." Kasey rang the buzzer for apartment four.

There was no response.

"Here, let me ring," Rinaldo said. "Maybe you didn't press hard enough."

Kasey let him give it a try, without commenting that muscles didn't really come into play when ringing door buzzers.

"I guess he's not here," she said finally. "If that's even him. I'm going to try apartment one."

"Good idea. That's probably the super."

The response came quickly, the high-pitched voice of a woman asking what they wanted.

"We're looking for Carl Dandridge," Kasey said into the intercom. "Can you help us?"

After a long silence, the buzzer rang, and they opened the door and went into the building. At the end of a long narrow hallway, a door opened halfway to reveal a tiny woman.

Kasey approached, Rinaldo at her side. "Are you the superintendent?"

"That's me. But if you're looking for Carl, he ain't in, honey. Sorry." She looked through the crack in the door with rheumy blue eyes.

"We'd like to wait for him, if that's possible. My name is Kasey Halliday. Carl used to work at Walk-by-Windows, where I'm acting manager."

"Yeah, I know the place you mean. Real fancy. Didn't quite suit Carl, seemed to me."

Kasey let that remark go by. "When do you expect he'll be back?"

"Never," the old woman said with a cackle.

"What do you mean?"

The woman smirked. "Carl don't live in this building anymore. He moved out."

"When?"

"Oh, four, no, five days ago." She ventured to open the door all the way. "Looks like that surprises you and your friend."

"Did he leave an address?"

"Sure did. Care of his sister out in California. She sent him a ticket. I saw it myself. Carl was glad to get out of New York, he said."

Kasey frowned in disbelief. "Are you sure he left five days ago?" It made no sense. The incident at the subway, the phone calls, the games at the restaurant, had all happened since then. "That can't be possible."

"I know what I know," the woman said firmly. "Carl don't live here anymore. He paid up his rent, packed his bags and moved to California. I already forwarded mail to him out there, and that's where he is." She crossed her arms over her bony chest almost triumphantly.

"Could I have his new address?" Kasey asked, still not willing to believe that Carl was gone.

"No, you cannot," the woman answered sharply. "If you want to reach Carl, write him a letter to this address and I'll be glad to forward it to him. Now I got things to do," she said, and before Kasey could respond, the woman closed the door.

"It's not fair," Rinaldo said as they headed for the waiting taxi.

Kasey didn't reply. She wasn't overly concerned that Rinaldo hadn't had the opportunity to show his prowess.

On the return trip to Walk-by-Windows, Kasey ignored Rinaldo's declarations about what he would have done if he'd got his hands on Carl, and attempted to rearrange the pieces of the puzzle inside her head.

The push at the subway station must have been accidental, as Will had suggested.

As for the other incidents, Carl could have called her long-distance and hung up. And he could have hired someone to order the lobsters, make the dinner reservations and raise hell in the bar. But that didn't sound like Carl. He usually acted on impulse and in the heat of anger.

All her instincts told her that when Carl moved to California, he cut his ties with New York, the restaurant and her. Sure, there was a possibility that he was behind the harassment, but in Kasey's opinion the chances were slim.

So if Carl *wasn't* responsible, what the hell was going on?

SHE DIDN'T HAVE TIME to ponder that question or anything else during the next few hours.

"You won't believe any of this," Judy said when Kasey returned to Windows. "Between the wholesaler's truck driver and our sous-chef, the lobster debacle was more than solved."

"Great," Kasey said. Then she saw Judy's face.

"It was reversed. The driver misunderstood his instructions and took away the entire order, including the lobster Albert was planning to cook."

"Oh, no," Kasey said.

"Yep. He can't fill any more orders for Lobster Albert. And he's ready to blow a fuse. The waiters are calling out the orders from the door instead of taking them into the kitchen," Judy told Kasey. "They're afraid to go in there, and I don't blame them."

Kasey managed to act as go-between for the rest of the evening, leaving her post only to straighten out two mixed-up orders and soothe a patron who arrived too late and missed his usual table. Run-of-the-mill stuff, Kasey knew, but in her state of mind, it was unsettling.

It was after eleven when Kasey searched out Judy in the bar. The last tables were being served coffee and dessert and everything seemed manageable. "Can you and Rinaldo lock up, Judy? I'm beat."

Judy looked up from the receipts spread out before her. "Sure, but I thought maybe we could share a taxi and talk. Some weird things are going on, Kasey."

"Tomorrow," Kasey promised.

"Then I'll wait with you until you get a cab. Is it still raining?"

"Last time I looked." Kasey picked up her raincoat and the two women stepped outside into the hot, humid night. The air was heavy with moisture, and streetlights glowed eerily in the darkness.

"I'd rather get soaked than swelter in this raincoat," Kasey said, pulling it off.

"It's just misting, anyway," Judy said. "And we're in luck." A taxi pulled up at the curb, its driver managing to create a spray of rainwater.

"I think they do that on purpose, but at this point I don't care," Kasey said, opening the back door.

"It's not the rain I'm worried about," Judy told her. "Be careful."

Kasey climbed in. "What could possibly happen between here and my apartment?"

"I don't know, but just to be safe, ask the driver to go around the block and let you out right in front of the building. It'll cost an extra seventy-five cents, but I'll feel better."

Kasey gave the driver her address, added Judy's suggestion and waved to her friend. She felt ill at ease, and Judy's fears hadn't helped.

At the first stoplight, a man rushed toward them and tried to open Kasey's door. She locked it quickly and slid across the seat to the other side. "Go on," she admonished the driver. "Get away from here!"

He turned around. "Lady, I got a red light. Wha'dya want me to do?"

"Change lanes at least—someone's trying to get in."

"Look again, lady."

Through the fogged-up window, she could see the man walking away.

"It's been raining, in case you hadn't noticed. The guy didn't see I got a fare. So, now can I obey the traffic lights or you got some more demands?"

Kasey didn't answer. She had enough on her mind. She didn't need to get involved in an argument with the cabdriver, too. The things Judy had referred to were definitely weird—and disconcerting. Even frightening. But something else was on her mind now.

After their wonderful night together, she hadn't heard from Will all day. While that shouldn't have taken precedence over her other problems, somehow it did.

As directed, the driver went around the block so he could deposit Kasey right in front of her building. She paid and got out, feeling safe with the ubiquitous Tim watching from his doorman's post.

She responded with as much animation as possible to his greeting and got on the elevator, praying for a problem-free ride to her floor. Her prayers answered, she got off at nineteen and headed to her apartment.

Will was standing at her door, leaning against the wall, arms crossed, waiting for her.

"Will—"

"Welcome home."

She was both pleased and confused. "How did you know when I'd be here?"

"That's a mystery, isn't it?"

For some reason, his remark gave her a little chill. She tried to ignore it. "No, really, Will. How did you know?"

He reached out and pulled her to him, giving her a hungry kiss. "I'm psychic."

"Will . . ."

He laughed and kissed her again. "Just joking, Kasey. My apartment looks out on Seventy-second Street, just like yours, remember? I saw you get out of the cab and immediately planted myself at your door."

"And I'm glad you did. I was wondering why I hadn't heard from you all day."

"I didn't want to bother you at work," he replied. "But work's over now so . . . May I come in?"

"I thought you'd never ask." Everything was all right now, Kasey thought. She was home safely and she was with Will.

The minute they got inside, he kissed her again. "Miss me?"

"Terribly," she replied, punctuating her answer with a kiss of her own. She stroked his beard. "It's nice, but—"

"But what?"

"But it's a little scratchy." She remembered Glenna's comment about the whisker burn on her cheeks. "One of these days, I'm going to shave it off," she said.

"Really?" He took her hand and led her down the hall.

"Yes. I have a fantasy of shaving you myself and see-ing your face for the first time—" She broke off. "Does that sound silly?"

"Sounds very interesting. The beard's beginning to bother me, too." He stroked it thoughtfully. "Maybe we can work something out." He sat down beside her in the living room. "Now tell me. How was your day—or your evening?"

"Awful. Until now," she amended. "It started with several crank phone calls—" Thinking that she felt Will stiffen, Kasey added hastily, "Nothing serious, just hang-ups. I was certain it was a weird guy who used to work at Windows. Turned out it wasn't."

"How do you know that?"

"Because he moved to California. I also thought he'd ordered the lobster—"

"You're losing me, Kasey. Lobster?"

Kasey sighed and leaned back against the sofa pillows. "I guess I need to bring you up to date."

"I guess so. Meanwhile, let me make you a drink." He laughed. "Listen to me, playing host in your place."

"It's okay. It's fine, in fact. There's white wine in the refrigerator. I'd love a glass. How about you?"

"Definitely." He disappeared into the kitchen, returning with two glasses and a bottle of cold white wine.

"About the lobster?" he asked, pouring the wine and passing a glass to her.

"The restaurant's order got horribly messed up and it took hours to straighten out. Then some woman started a ruckus in the bar—"

"And you thought this guy might have been behind it all? He must be a nut."

"Not a nut, just mean spirited and sneaky. But now I know Carl's not behind any of it. I'm beginning to think that everything was coincidence. Maybe the wholesaler made a mistake in the order and put the blame on someone else. And people get upset in restaurants all the time. As far as the hang-ups are concerned, wrong numbers happen. I think I was seeing a conspiracy where none existed." She settled into the crook of his arm. "I'd even wondered if Carl pushed me at the subway stop last night."

"You still think that was deliberate?"

"Not now. It was probably just an accident, a lot of people jostling on a platform."

"I think you're right, but let's face it, there are lots of crazy people around, Kasey. It pays to be careful."

There was an undercurrent in Will's voice that caught her attention. She glanced sharply up at him but couldn't read the veiled expression on his face.

"I know, but a certain amount of craziness is normal for the city. I guess I've been on edge recently, letting my imagination work overtime."

"I thought we'd worked all those tensions out last night. And this morning."

Kasey slipped her arm around his neck. "I may need an encore performance."

Will chuckled. "Delighted. I happen to be free tonight."

7

"WHAT WOULD YOU say to making love on the balcony?" Will asked, nuzzling Kasey's neck.

"On the balcony?"

"Just an idea. An erotic one. But then, all of my ideas about you are like that." He let his fingers trail along the curve of her back. "Now I'm thinking about your offer to shave off my beard."

"And?"

"I'm going to take you up on it."

Kasey smiled broadly.

"It goes along with my erotic thoughts, lying under your spell—and under your razor—helpless, your bearded slave."

"But we don't have to do it on the balcony?"

"Do it?" he asked.

"You know what I mean," she replied, taking a swipe at him. "Shave."

He laughed. "I suppose I can change my fantasy to an indoor version."

"We'll need towels and soap," she said.

"Do you really want to do this?" He asked the question while running his hands along her back.

She nodded.

"It's not going to be that simple. You'll probably have to start with scissors. Then a good razor. Shaving cream and—"

"Let's go to your apartment," Kasey suggested.

"No," he said quickly. "I'd rather stay here."

"I don't have shaving cream. Or the kind of razor we'll need," she told him.

"Okay." He got up, one hand still possessively touching her, drifting along her hip. "I'll get the supplies and bring them over here." He took her hand, and Kasey followed him to the end of the hall, where he gave her a quick kiss. "I'll be right back."

WILL CLOSED THE DOOR of his apartment, leaned back against it and took a slow deep breath. He was so caught up in the fantasy with Kasey that he hadn't taken time to think.

He ran his hand across his beard. It was driving him crazy. He hated it and resented the need for it, but was he ready to give it up? Common sense advised him to tell Kasey he'd changed his mind, but the twin demons of impatience and recklessness pushed him toward the decision.

Will went into the bathroom and switched on the light. He studied his face in the mirror. The beard made him a stranger, even to himself. He wanted it gone. Tonight. And he wanted Kasey to be the one to shave it off.

There was more to it than just getting a clean shave. It was also a beginning in revealing himself to Kasey. He still couldn't open himself to her completely, but this was a step. And if it brought danger his way, then so be it. He was fed up with living his life in the dark.

Quickly, before he could change his mind, Will loaded his kit with a couple of razors, a can of shaving cream and a bottle of after-shave. He found a pair of scissors and made a few passes at his beard. He'd help Kasey along but not make the task too easy. He wanted the experience to last. Satisfied with the start he'd made, he added the scissors to his supplies.

Then he reached into the drawer and dropped a packet of condoms into the kit, grinning at himself in the mirror. This was going to be a hell of a fantasy, and he was going to enjoy every minute of it.

Still smiling, he turned off the light and headed back to Kasey.

"I'M ALL YOURS." Will tilted back his head and closed his eyes.

Kasey's bathroom was bathed in soft light. Reflections from the recessed lighting glowed in the smoky floor-to-ceiling mirrors. The rain had started again and beat softly against the window panes.

Kasey began to shave Will, leaning forward and moving the razor carefully across his cheek. She was wrapped in a towel, knotted above her breasts and skimming the tops of her thighs. Her clothes—and Will's—lay strewn across the bedroom floor, tossed carelessly aside as they'd hurriedly undressed each other, eager to begin their fantasy.

Will was seated on the edge of the tub, a towel draped across his lap. Kasey was very aware of his nearness—and his nakedness. The atmosphere was intimate, provocative. Anticipation shimmered on the hot, heavy air.

Kasey wiped away a drop of shaving cream that had splattered on Will's shoulder. Under his warm and pliant skin, she could feel the tightening and tensing of his muscles. Excitement tingled along Kasey's spine, and she took a deep breath to steady her shaking hand.

They were both quiet, the patter of rain and the scraping of the razor on Will's skin the only sounds to be heard. Kasey was into a rhythm now, almost as if her movements were choreographed, gliding the razor along his face, rinsing it off, and then leaning close to him again, so close that the heat from his body mingled with her own. And that heat had nothing to do with the summer night.

Just as she slid the razor along the line of his chin, Will opened his eyes and looked directly at her.

She nicked him. "Damn. I'm sorry," she said.

"No problem. I'll carry the scar with pleasure, and always think of you."

Kasey laughed. "It's only a tiny nick, Will. I don't think there'll be a scar."

"Too bad," he said, closing his eyes again.

She tipped his chin back and shaved his neck, washed off the razor and carefully went over the spots she'd missed. "Okay, here goes the mustache." Slowly, inch by inch, she shaved his upper lip. As she wiped away the traces of shaving cream, Will's features began to emerge—his high cheekbones, the sensuous curve of his mouth, his strong chin.

She caught her breath and stared at him. Her fantasy was close, so close . . .

"Finished?" Will sounded impatient.

"Not quite," Kasey replied, tearing her eyes away from him. "You need the full treatment." She soaked a washcloth in hot water, wrung it out and carefully placed it over his face. It was part of the treatment, all right, but it also gave her a chance to slow her racing heart. Will was even more handsome than she'd imagined.

After a minute, she removed the washcloth, and wiped away the remaining shaving cream.

She stepped back, staring, letting herself take in the full picture of the "naked" Will. "You're beautiful," she said.

Opening his eyes, Will replied, "Men aren't beautiful, Kasey."

"You are." She leaned forward and kissed his cleanly shaven cheek, running her lips along his smooth, damp, sweet-smelling face. Then she kissed his chin. Then his mouth. "If you only knew how good that feels."

"I know how good *this* feels." He tugged once at her towel and it dropped away.

She could feel the heat of Will's gaze on her bare skin. Her breasts felt hot and heavy, swollen with desire, aching for his touch. He cupped her breasts with his hand and took one taut nipple slowly into his mouth. Dizzying desire swept through Kasey at the touch of his lips, at the warm wetness of his mouth and tongue. Her hands played through the crisp texture of his hair, drawing him closer to her.

Will surged to his feet, letting his towel drop to the floor. His mouth was hard on hers. She moaned with pleasure.

"I want to make love to you, Kasey. Here, now."

"Here? Now?"

Will laughed and pulled her down on the softness of the rug. He ran his hand down her arm and pressed a condom into her hand.

"Put it on me, Kasey. I want you to touch me. I want you to see how ready I am for you."

With eager fingers, Kasey slid the rubber down along his hard, throbbing manhood. Then she lay back and guided him toward her, her legs apart to welcome him.

He wrapped his arms around her shoulders, and slid into her. Kasey's body stiffened with excitement and she dug her nails into the muscles of his shoulders. She felt on fire, consumed by her need for him. His mouth captured hers and their breaths mingled, his tongue moving slowly, sensuously in and out of her mouth as he moved in and out of her body.

The mirrored bathroom wall reflected every move they made. "Open your eyes, Kasey," Will asked. "Look at us, watch us in the mirror. Watch us make love. Watch us make our fantasy come true."

Kasey thought that she had known desire before in her life. But everything that had gone before seemed a prelude as she looked into the mirror and saw their hot, eager bodies join in the act of love.

KASEY ZIPPED UP her jeans and reached for her tennis shoes beside the bed. Will's hand shot out from under the sheet and grabbed her wrist. "Hey, running out on me so early in the morning?"

Kasey sank beside him and pushed his hair away from his forehead. She loved the way he looked without his beard. There was a trace of stubble across his face, but it didn't hide his cheeks, high-boned with hollows beneath them, his square chin with its faint dimple, his strong jaw and wide shapely mouth.

"Kasey?" he asked, breaking into her reverie.

"Oh, sorry. I was just enjoying the new you."

He laughed. "I love your honesty. But if you're so mesmerized, why are you running out on me so early in the morning?"

"I'm running out to the bakery and the newsstand." She let her fingers trail down across his cheek, down his neck to his shoulder. His skin was pliant under her touch, and she remembered the long, wonderful night when she'd held him close and moved her hands over his skin. Then it had been hot with passion; now it was warm and comforting. She sighed happily. There was nothing quite like waking up with Will. She could easily get used to it. "I thought we could lounge around, ease into the day with the paper and pastries."

"That sounds good for starters," he murmured as he raised her hand to his lips and kissed her palm. "But I have other ideas about the way we can spend a rainy morning in New York."

Kasey gave him a kiss on the cheek and finished lacing her shoes. "Not exactly rainy, but very cloudy. And I want to spend the morning the same way."

"Oh? And what way is that?"

She laughed. "What were you thinking?"

"You tell me first."

"Something like last night," she said, blushing in spite of herself as she got up and went to the window. "Yes, it's definitely cloudy out there."

Will stretched his arms above his head. "You're all the sunshine I need. Hurry back, Kasey."

THERE WAS A SMILE on her face when she breezed past Tim, out the door and down the street. She liked the image behind Will's words. She was the sunshine of his life. Bringing light to dark corners.

She slowed down as she approached Broadway, confused by her own thoughts, wondering why she would assume that Will had dark corners in his life. Just because he was a little secretive . . . Well, more than a little. But in time, she'd learn everything about him, dark corners and all.

She stopped to buy the morning paper from Mike.

"Glad to get a little rain last night. Hope it'll cool things off," Mike offered, spouting his usual early-morning weather commentary. "But I'm afraid today's just gonna be another hot and steamy one soon's the sun comes out."

Kasey crossed the street, trying to hide her grin. The weather outside couldn't compare to the situation in her apartment, which was *really* hot and steamy.

Gina Fenelli stood behind the counter of the bakery, which was momentarily empty, and greeted Kasey with a smile. "We have a break, and I can't think of anything better than filling it with you. Thought you'd deserted us, Kasey."

"Never," Kasey vowed. "I've just been busy the last few mornings. But today I'm going to make up for all the treats I've missed. I'd like half a dozen pastries, all of them wonderful, of course."

Gina rolled her eyes knowingly. "So. Sharing with your neighbor again. It's a man, right? A boyfriend? How'd he like the special raspberry hazelnut torte I gave you last time?"

"Actually he's more of a chocolate man. So could you be sure to include a chocolate croissant." Kasey thought about Will's seemingly incompatible tastes. Chocolate pastries and hot dogs. Silk shirts and the best wines. He was never predictable and never boring.

"You like this man, eh? I can tell by the look in your eyes when you talk about him," Gina said as she chose a variety of pastries, deftly removing them from the glass case and assembling them in a pink bakery box.

"He's very nice." Kasey tried to remain cool but failed. "In fact, he's wonderful, Gina. So good-looking and smart and funny." It wasn't like her to go on and on about a man. But then Will wasn't just *any* man.

Gina wrapped string around the box, cut it and looked up at Kasey, her eyes twinkling. "So, when do I meet Mr. Wonderful? Bring him in. I'll give him a treat right from the oven."

"I will, very soon. He lives at—" Kasey broke off in midsentence. Will was so reticent about his life, so protective of his privacy, that she felt guilty gossiping about him. "How much do I owe you?" she asked quickly, digging into her pockets.

Gina gave Kasey the total and, busy with the sale, didn't seem to notice the unfinished sentence.

"You bring him by so the Fenelli family can pass approval on him."

"I will," Kasey promised, scooting out the door as another customer entered.

"I WILL," she repeated to herself, "when he and I adjust to . . ." Adjust to what, she wondered. Being in love? Being a couple? Maybe they needed to talk; there was so much she didn't know, but Will had a way of changing the subject whenever she wanted to talk about him—his family, his work . . . his past.

Kasey breezed through the lobby of Bartow Tower, trying to figure out a way to get Will to open up to her.

Maybe being direct was best.

She pushed the elevator button and looked around for Tim. His post was empty. "So much for the security of Bartow Tower," she muttered to herself.

As she stepped off the elevator on the nineteenth floor, Tim was standing in the hall.

"I was hoping I'd see you, Ms. Halliday. I rang your buzzer. I was sure I heard someone inside and thought maybe Mr. Eastman..." He let that remark hang in the air. "But no one answered."

"No," Kasey repeated. Will must have had his own reason for not responding.

"I wanted to tell you that there's a new tenant on your floor." Tim stepped aside and Kasey caught her first view of an elderly woman in a wheelchair.

"This is Mrs. Janek. She's renting 1901." Tim's eyes sought out Kasey's pleadingly. "I need to get back to the lobby. Would you mind getting her settled in?"

"Well, I—" Kasey couldn't give away Will's presence and she didn't have another excuse handy. "Sure, I'll help."

"How nice of you, dear." Mrs. Janek's voice was soft but steady. "It's so difficult getting moved in, isn't it? Now, what did Tim call you? Holiday, was it?"

"Halliday, but call me Kasey."

"I'm Freya Janek." The woman held out her hand as Tim stepped onto the elevator with a wave.

Kasey shook hands, trying not to stare at Mrs. Janek's attire. Gloves in August? Her dress was long-sleeved, full and flowing, and she wore a big hat. Kasey couldn't get a handle on her exact age, but she seemed to be a spectre from another century.

"I can usually manage by myself, but I do need help with these bags." She gestured to the overnight cases at her feet. "My cosmetics. I wouldn't entrust them to movers."

Kasey sighed and picked up the luggage, hoping to get this episode over quickly. She wished that she'd never gained a reputation as the building house-mother. But she had. And there was nothing she could do about it except help the poor woman.

Mrs. Janek struggled with her key and finally unlocked the door to 1901. Her motorized wheelchair made a soft whirring sound as Kasey followed her down the hall, past the closed bedroom door to the living room, which was almost empty. A table, a chair, a telephone. The place was depressingly bare, four freshly painted white walls and curtainless balcony doors revealing gray skies outside.

Mrs. Janek waved a gloved hand at the room. "My furniture is being reupholstered. It seemed the perfect time. New apartment, fresh start in life. You know, my dear, one is never too old to begin again."

"I like that attitude." Kasey noticed that the elderly woman had a slight accent. European, she surmised, imagining that Mrs. Janek had once lived grandly. Eccentric but interesting, she'd be a nice addition to the floor, Kasey realized. She probably had fascinating stories to tell.

"Shall I put your luggage in the bedroom?" she asked.

"No, just leave everything here. I'll unpack gradually. I'm used to taking care of myself and I try not to let this wheelchair slow me down. I've had hip surgery, you see, but I'm healing very nicely," she confided. "I'll be out of this chair soon."

"If there's anything I can do to help you until then, just let me know. I realize moving in can be a hassle." Kasey edged toward the hall, eager to get back to Will.

"You're so kind. Have you lived here long?"

"One year."

"And do you like Bartow Tower? Now be honest, please."

Kasey chose her words carefully. "The building has a lot of nice features. Storage facilities, laundry room, parking garage. And when the weather's sunny, these balconies are lovely." She skipped the stories about stalled elevators and power outages. No point in upsetting Mrs. Janek unnecessarily. Besides, if she got into all that, she'd never get out of here.

"What about security? A single woman has to be so careful. Are you alone, too, dear?"

Kasey nodded and thought about last night when she hadn't been alone at all. She'd been with Will, sleeping next to him all night, her body curled into his. Actually, although she didn't let Mrs. Janek know it, she'd never felt less alone in her life.

"Security is pretty good. There's always a doorman on duty. As far as I know, we've never had a break-in here." In spite of all the other problems, that much was true.

"I feel much safer hearing that, although I plan to keep my door double-locked just in case. What about these balconies?"

"The only intruder you'll have is the neighbor's cat. Lo Mein will probably be checking you out soon. He's a nosy Siamese who prowls the balconies."

"How charming. I love animals. Perhaps I'll get a cat of my own." She peered up at Kasey through tinted glasses. "But here I am talking away as if we had all day. I'm probably holding you up."

There was her break, Kasey thought. "Yes, I—"

"But if you could just do me one favor."

"Of course." Kasey tried not to grimace.

"In the kitchen. My coffeepot is plugged in and ready to start brewing my favorite blend. But I simply can't open the coffee can. My hands, you know," she added without revealing the exact problem.

Kasey assumed it was arthritis. "I'll open it for you." She headed for the kitchen. Start the coffee brewing and then you're out of here, she told herself.

In a matter of minutes, Kasey had the coffeepot perking away and as an exit line decided to offer Mrs. Janek a bakery treat. "I have some pastries here. Shall I leave you one?"

"Oh, my dear, that would be lovely. You don't have anything chocolate, do you? I'm addicted, I must admit."

Kasey only hesitated a moment before lying expertly. "No, I'm sorry. But I do have a wonderful almond torte. Would you like that?"

"Yes, thank you very much. I'm lucky to have such a thoughtful neighbor. Lucky but not surprised. Tim said I'd like you. You'll have to come over sometime and tell me all about the rest of the people on this floor. I bet you know everyone."

"That's my reputation. I'll be glad to introduce you around."

"When you have the time, my dear. I'm sure you're very busy. You work during the day?"

"Well, no. Actually I'm with Walk-by-Windows down on Columbus Circle. I don't go in until midafternoon, so anytime you need anything, just let me know." Kasey bit her lip, wondering what it was about her personality that made her reveal herself completely to total strangers. Judy would be giving her a warning about now. Well, she thought, at least the woman wasn't a threat.

"I'll remember your kind offer," Mrs. Janek told her. "You don't know how good it makes me feel."

As Kasey managed her exit, the elderly woman called after her, "You'll be hearing from me, my dear."

KASEY TRIED not to think of what Mrs. Janek had in mind as she let herself into her apartment. One of these days, she'd stop being everyone's friend.

Will was in the kitchen pouring a cup of coffee. He'd pulled on his trousers, but his chest was bare, and his hair was still tousled from the night before.

"I was about to go out and look for you. Where did you go for the pastries, Paris?"

Kasey laughed. "I got tied up." She stood for a moment gazing at him, feeling a warm glow of contentment. He looked so different without his beard. More vulnerable, less mysterious, but just as handsome. She and Will were characters in a very intimate scene, she thought. Two lovers, the morning after, sharing coffee.

She took the cup he offered, gave him a quick kiss and handed him the box of pastries. "Your chocolate pastry was almost stolen away, but I managed to hand over an almond one, instead."

"Don't tell me you were held up, and the thief only got away with an almond croissant."

"It was a torte, actually, and I gave it away."

Will opened the box. "Ah-ha. Here's the chocolate. All safe and sound." He took a bite. "And delicious. Now, let's see… How about a cinnamon twist for you?"

She accepted the pastry.

"So tell me about your adventure. Who almost stole my croissant?"

"Our neighbor. Freya Janek. I helped her move in."

"Another new tenant. What's she like?"

Kasey leaned against the kitchen counter, trying to analyze his curious look. "Could that be interest I see in your eyes? I'm not sure I like that."

"Don't tell me you're jealous."

"You'd be surprised," Kasey replied. "The other day when Glenna came over and told me you'd been to her apartment—"

Will stopped in midbite. "Wait a minute. I was never in Glenna's apartment."

"I know. But I thought you were. You returned Lo Mein to her, and when she told me about it, I got a little jealous. That isn't like me at all," she added. "I'm not the obsessive type. Or at least I never have been. But that stab of jealousy almost scared me."

She couldn't quite read the look that passed over his face before he spoke, quickly and decisively. "You're not obsessive, Kasey. You're the most open and honest person I know. And I'm flattered that you were jealous. Even a little bit."

"Glenna is a great-looking woman," Kasey ventured.

"Sure, if you like long-legged brunettes." He pulled Kasey close and kissed her. "I prefer petite blondes with nice firm bodies and wild imaginations."

"Good, I'm relieved." She smiled at him. "So let's finish the pastries and then—"

"And then? Let our imaginations run wild?"

"I don't have to be at work until four o'clock. That gives us a whole morning and part of the afternoon. I, um, thought we might talk for a while."

"Talk? We talk all the time, Kasey. Even in bed."

She looked up at him through lowered lashes.

He smiled. "Sure we do, a suggestive word here and there." He let his fingers drift provocatively along her cheek.

"That's not what I mean, Will. I mean, really talk," Kasey persisted. "I know so little about you, and I want to know more."

"It's a long story. Are you sure you have time to hear it? Or will you be running errands for the new gal down the the hall—what did you say she was like?"

Distracted, Kasey chuckled. "Well, first of all, she's no gal, although she might like the description. She's an older woman, exactly how old, I can't say. Her face was pretty wrinkled, but her eyes looked unusually young behind very thick, tinted glasses."

"So she's elderly?"

"Definitely a senior citizen."

Kasey thought she saw a look of relief pass over Will's face. "Oh, and she's temporarily wheelchair-bound, which was why I had to give her a hand."

"That's too bad," Will responded.

"She seems to handle it pretty well. And she's very cultivated. A European background, I think. I'll introduce you."

Will gave her a hug. "Nope. I know everyone on the nineteenth floor I want to know. You're the woman for me."

"Prove it," Kasey challenged, wrapping her arms around his waist.

"Are you trying to seduce me, Kasey Halliday?"

"I might be." She insinuated herself against him. "And I won't tell Tim if you don't."

Will stiffened. "What in the world does that mean?"

"It means Tim is back at his post."

He was silent.

"And leaving us alone," she added. "He rang the buzzer a while ago, looking for me."

"That was Tim?"

"Yes. I thought you probably saw him through the peephole in the door . . ."

"No," he said quickly. "I didn't bother to go to the door. Figured it was one of your nineteenth-floor fans."

"It might have been me," she teased.

"Oh, no." He gave her another hug, relaxed and easy. "You aren't the type to forget your keys. You're much too focused."

"Is that good?" she asked, forgetting about Tim and the problem he seemed to present to Will.

"Of course. All of your traits are good. Especially the tendency you have to talk about one thing while doing another."

She frowned at him. "Explain, please."

"Well, you're talking about the doorman and making love to me."

"Making love?"

"Yes, everything you do to me and with me is a kind of lovemaking. Like right now. You're slipping your hands around my hips. I'm not even sure you realize you're doing it, but you're driving me crazy."

"You have nice hips," she said. "Tight and trim but very accessible."

Will pulled up her T-shirt. "Just as you're accessible to me. Mmm," he added, "no bra. That makes undressing you a lot easier." He reached for her zipper just as she reached for his—or started to.

"What about your life story?" she asked, pulling a little away from him.

He took a firm grip on her hand and moved it back to his zipper.

"You're doing it again," she murmured. "Changing the subject."

"*This* is the subject, Kasey," he told her.

"I think you're right," she answered, giving herself over to her feelings as they slipped their hands inside each other's jeans, stroking warm, eager flesh, causing a delicious heat, slow and thick as honey, to flood through both of them.

Will's breath was moist against her ear. "We'll talk soon. I swear. But for now . . ."

Kasey was already lost in a haze of need. How could it be possible, she wondered, to want him so much, to need him all of the time? She kept wondering that as they worked their way out of their jeans and he pulled off her shirt.

Naked, they wrapped themselves in each other's arms. Kasey ran her hands up the muscles of his back, along his neck, and threaded her fingers through his thick hair. Their lips met in a long thorough kiss, and she thought that this was the way love should be. Two people in total harmony, giving and taking, sharing themselves.

There was nothing in Kasey's memory of her life's experience that could compare with the feelings that coursed through her as their naked bodies entwined.

His erection pushed against her; their groins rubbed together, and his legs wrapped around hers. Standing together, they were closer to making love than it was possible to be and still not be joined.

Suddenly, Will reached down and scooped her into his arms. "I'm taking you back to bed, Kasey. Any objections?"

She covered his mouth with hers, and when the kiss ended, whispered just one word, "Hurry."

THE AFTERNOON SUN broke through the clouds and bathed the room in a soft hazy glow. Will awakened first and lay quiet, not wanting to disturb Kasey. A strand of her golden hair lay across his shoulder; he could feel her warm breath against his skin. She slept deeply, her face relaxed, her lashes dark shadows against her cheeks.

She looked young and vulnerable, yet the soft line of her hip and the fullness of her breasts that curved against his body were womanly and seductive. What a mix Kasey was, both an innocent and a temptress. As soon as he thought he knew her, another layer of her personality was revealed, piquing his desire to know more.

She was more caring than anyone he'd ever known. She wore her heart on her sleeve, and that was a part of her charm—honesty and candor in a world of cynicism and lies. Ask anything of her and she'd be there to give, to help. He thought of their new neighbor, who had already discovered that Kasey was an easy touch. Kasey would probably be running frequent errands for the old gal.

But that was only one facet of Kasey's personality— the desire to reach out to everyone. He was discovering a secret side of her, something wild, free and unexpected that smoldered with fantasy and imagination.

He'd been blown away by her responsiveness from the first time they'd made love. Her passion and intensity had matched his, and together they'd reached a level of intimacy that he'd never felt before. He'd even let her shave his beard, although he knew that was risky. But it was what Kasey had wanted, and he'd been happy to oblige.

Will touched her face lightly with his finger, loving the feel of her skin, soft, creamy and utterly kissable.

She stirred, and he was sure he saw a smile curve her lips. He wondered what she was dreaming about. He wanted to know all her dreams and fantasies; he wanted to be part of them.

Will closed his eyes and thought about his life and the games he had recently been forced to play. Everything was growing more and more complex. And Kasey was part of the complication. He needed to tell her everything that had happened before they met, everything that was happening now. And what could happen next.

But when—and how—could he tell her? God, he was a bastard, but he'd warned her of that the first day they'd spent together. He'd told her in the park that he was selfish and spoiled. He'd put her off and tried to stay away from her. But she'd ignored all the warnings. She'd come to him, open and loving, and for all his resolve, he couldn't keep away from her.

As Will lay beside her, listening to her soft, even breathing, feeling the delicious warmth of her body, he knew that he couldn't let her go. But he also knew that he had to tell her what was going on. And he would. Soon.

8

KASEY'S BODY still glowed with the warmth of Will's lovemaking when she reached the newsstand the next morning. Her face was still flushed with the memory as she picked up her afternoon paper. But halfway to Walk-by-Windows, something else grabbed her attention. That something was Mattison Monroe.

Before she reached Columbus Circle, Kasey had opened the paper to the restaurant section and stopped in her tracks. There it was—Mattison's review! She waited at the light and skimmed the article, looking for superlatives and finding them. It was a rave.

She bought three more copies of the paper at the newsstand on the corner outside Windows and dropped one of them on the reservations desk under Judy's nose.

"We're a hit," she declared. "Have you seen this? Page six, second section. He loved it."

"Who? What?" Judy thumbed through the paper.

"Mattison. The lobster."

Judy caught on and squealed with glee. "He loved it?"

"Absolutely adored the dish and said some nice things about the restaurant, too."

Judy found the article and read it quickly. "Nothing about service! Why would the color of the tablecloths be more important than the quality of the service?"

"You are absolutely the most pessimistic person I know," Kasey said. "Reviews aren't all that long, Judy. A food critic can't cover everything. Besides, judging from this praise, he'll want to come back and try other dishes."

"Hmm."

"Besides, he didn't say the service was bad, did he?"

Judy grinned. "Nope, he didn't. I guess that's a plus I can pass on to the staff. As for Albert and Fred, they'll be out of their heads with joy. Albert will forgive you for the lobster debacle, and Fred will be ecstatic. This will be good for you, too. After all, Mattison's rave happened on your watch."

"Which is almost over, thank God. Fred's due back in two days, and then I'm free. Maybe I can get some time off." She pulled Judy over to their predinner table. "Can I tell you something?"

Judy was still lost in the review. "Sure. But we need to have this laminated and framed before Fred gets back. We can hang it in the entranceway, and—"

"Judy, listen to me, this is important."

"I know, that's why we should get it framed today, tomorrow at the latest."

"OK. I'll take care of it. Now sit down." Kasey pulled her friend into a seat and brought her chair up beside her.

"This is about me, not Windows," she said.

"Oh?" Judy leaned toward Kasey. "Tell all."

"If you'll listen and not overreact."

"Me, overreact?" Judy rolled her eyes toward the ceiling. "I can't imagine why you'd say that."

Kasey sighed deeply and signaled for Mack to bring their usual ice tea. "Because I'm talking about me—and Will."

The corners of Judy's mouth turned down. "Surprise, surprise." She gave herself a little shake. "Sorry. I said I'd listen and I will. You look very serious."

"I *am* very serious, Judy. I'm falling in love—no, that's not true. I'm already in love with him. Wildly, totally. He's the most wonderful, the sexiest . . . You should see him now, Judy. I shaved off his beard—"

"You what?"

"Shaved his beard," Kasey said, accepting her ice tea from Mack and taking a sip.

"What kind of games are you two playing?"

Kasey didn't even blush. "Lovers' games. And this is for real."

Judy's usually mobile face was suddenly serious, her brown eyes shaded with worry. "I might as well admit that I've been expecting this—and worrying about it. Why?" She answered her own question. "Because you know practically nothing about him."

"I know all I need to know."

"Oh, yeah?" Judy asked doubtfully, sitting back and sipping her tea. "Specifics, please."

"He's wonderfully supportive. I feel safe with him." When Judy didn't react, she added, "After the subway incident, I was really dependent on Will, and he was there, protective and—"

Judy put up a warning hand. "Slow down. What subway incident?"

"Oh, it was nothing, really. When we left your party, we ran into a crazy crowd of partiers on the subway platform. When the train came, I was bumped and almost fell on the track. At the time, I thought someone had pushed me."

"My God, that's awful!"

"But Will grabbed me and pulled me away. If it hadn't been for him, well, I hate to think what would have happened."

"Someone pushed you?"

"I thought I felt a hand on my back, and for a moment I teetered there on the edge. But now I'm convinced it was accidental."

"What changed your mind?"

"Frankly?" Kasey thought that over for a moment. "I believe it was Carl's move to California. Before I knew that he was on the other side of the country, I thought he might have done it. Remember, I was sure Carl made the phone calls."

"And screwed up things here," Judy reminded her.

"But it turns out that he couldn't have been responsible. And now I believe everything was in my mind."

"Yeah." Judy studied Kasey with narrowed eyes. "I guess so. But doesn't it seem weird to you that *all* those strange things happened recently?"

"Well . . ."

"You really believe it's coincidence?" Judy prodded.

"As Will says, there are a lot of crazy people out there."

"And all the crazy people seem to be hanging around you. But they've only been hanging around for the past week or so."

"I guess. Maybe a little longer."

"Only since you met Will Eastman."

Kasey opened her mouth to reply, but Judy kept on talking, her voice deadly serious. "Item one, you met him under suspicious circumstances on the elevator. Just over a week ago, if I'm not mistaken."

"Fate," Kasey replied.

"Later, you were locked in the storage room with him."

"Fate again. Wonderful, romantic fate."

"The lobster screwup wasn't so romantic," Judy said.

"That had nothing to do with—"

"But it happened in the same time frame, Kasey," Judy reminded her. "So did the reservations mess, the phone calls and the subway push. All since you met Will Eastman."

Kasey couldn't help getting angry. She took a deep breath to avoid a confrontation with Judy and spoke evenly. "Why would Will harass me like that? It makes no sense."

"Unless . . ." Judy was thoughtful. "Unless he was playing a game with you."

"Not Will—"

"Give me a chance to explain, Kasey."

"All right, but you'll never convince me."

"Let's say he harasses you, gives you a hard time. You get nervous, uptight. Then he steps in to save you. Mr. Wonderful, offering to make everything right."

"Will didn't—"

Judy leaned forward and faced Kasey directly. "That's what happened, isn't it?"

Kasey thought back to the first time they'd made love. After the subway incident. She'd been keyed up, on edge and desperately vulnerable. And he'd been there for her. "Those may be the facts," she admitted, "but they don't mean a thing."

"I think they do, Kasey. I always had a strange feeling about the guy, and his pursuit of you proves I was right."

"Ha!" Kasey said victoriously. "There you're wrong. I was the one who pursued Will. I wanted him, Judy. I asked him to lunch in the park. I invited him to your party. I knocked on his door—"

Judy gave a dismissive shake of her head. "That's the oldest come-on in the book, and you know it. He plays hard to get, and you go after him. He's messing with your head, Kasey. I think he's dangerous."

Kasey didn't reply immediately, and for a good reason. The word *dangerous* had got to her. She remembered the feeling of fear that had overcome her during those first moments on the elevator with Will. Danger. It had been her first impression of him. She'd felt it again in the storage room. Getting to know him, she'd shed her apprehension. But first impressions could sometimes be lasting ones.

Kasey came to her senses. "This is ridiculous, Judy. Whatever I thought of Will when I first met him doesn't matter. I know him now and he's nothing like your description. You make him sound like some kind of nut case when he's really a wonderful, intelligent and loving man—"

"Who lurks around dark corners, doesn't show his face in the daylight, runs from TV cameras and has tons of money but no job." Judy sat back, gloating. "I rest my case. And add another thought to it. Maybe he's a psychopath."

"Judy, this is insane."

"You could be living next door to a mental case, and falling in love with him!" Her eyes lit up. "I know! Let's hire a private detective to check him out."

Kasey burst into laughter. "Hire a detective? Absolutely not."

Judy shrugged and finished her tea. "It's not so crazy. Lots of women hire detectives."

"Not me," Kasey said decisively.

"If you won't hire a private eye, then let's get my uncle Paul."

Kasey was laughing again.

"No, listen to me. He's at the Department of Motor Vehicles. He can run a check on Will. Or what about this—my friend Rachel's husband is a cop. He could look into the records—"

"No, no, no. You're the crazy one now, Judy. First, you were sure that Will's ex-wife was harassing me. Now you're sure Will himself is the harasser."

"If not Will or his wife, then who, Kasey? Who has it in for you?"

"Could be anyone. Some disgruntled patron..."

"Yeah, sure. Someone whose soufflé fell flat. Those people usually resort to harassment," Judy said sarcastically.

"Maybe that redheaded woman," Kasey offered. "She's been causing problems."

"Oh, get real. A customer never would go to such extremes."

Kasey thought hurriedly. "What about Glenna! You know, the woman on my floor. She's very interested in Will. Maybe she's jealous," Kasey said, trying to remember that early-morning conversation with Glenna. "I got the first phone call just after I told her about Will and me."

"Now look who sounds crazy," Judy said. "The woman you're describing is the one who's never without a man, the one who goes away weekends and leaves you to baby-sit her cat. Be serious, Kasey. Does Glenna sound like a jealous lunatic?"

"No," Kasey said honestly. "She doesn't. Besides, she and I are friends. I'm just grabbing at straws, trying to come up with suspects to get you off Will's case. But I don't need to do that because Will has nothing—"

"Maybe not. But there's a way to be sure," Judy said excitedly. "You could turn sleuth yourself, get into his apartment, go through his stuff and find out what he's all about!"

"I'd never do that," Kasey said adamantly. "Besides, I've only been in his apartment once."

"That's strange, too. Look at me and Danny. I go to his place, he comes to mine. I know his folks, he knows mine. I've even seen his high school yearbook and met most of his friends."

"And you've known Danny for a long time. Will and I are just beginning. All of that will come later."

"Not if you don't help it along," Judy warned darkly. "You've got to find out about this man, Kasey. You owe it to yourself. But be very careful."

BEING CAREFUL was one thing, spending extra taxi fare to go around the block every night was another. Kasey got off on the corner. All she had to do was cross the street and walk home. But instead of checking for cars and then dashing across when there was a break in traffic, as she usually did, she stood patiently on the corner, waiting for the light.

When the light changed, Kasey stepped into the street. Judy's warning must have lodged in her mind because she found herself pausing again, looking over her shoulder before turning to check the side street.

That's when she saw the car bearing down on her like a four-wheeled monster. With a shriek, she jumped backward out of its path, stumbled on the curb and fell in a sprawl on the edge of the sidewalk. The car skidded around the corner, so close that she could smell the burning tire rubber.

"Oh, my God, lady, you were almost hit." A young couple appeared out of nowhere. The man bent over to help her up.

"Be careful," the woman cautioned. "She may be hurt. Are you all right?"

"I think so," Kasey said shakily. She realized then that she was trembling all over, and her legs hardly seemed able to support her. She held on to the man's arm and leaned against him, taking a deep breath to calm her pounding heart. She'd been inches away from death. "Nothing broken," she said weakly as she tried to avoid collapsing.

The woman stepped over and took her other arm, steadying her. "These city drivers are insane. They never look where they're going. I was almost hit just last week." She spoke to the man. "Did you get the license number, honey?"

"No way," he said. "That character was going too fast. I couldn't even make out the car model. A dark sedan, and I'd swear there were no headlights.

"Probably burned out and not replaced. Too many clunkers on the street with uninsured, unlicensed drivers at the wheel. It's a disgrace. The city ought to do something about it—"

"The police have their hands full with crime in the streets," the man told her before turning his attention to Kasey. "Can we walk you home?"

"No, I can make it. I'm fine, thank you." She was, except for her torn stockings, pounding heart and the embarrassment of falling flat on her face in front of an audience.

But the couple insisted on crossing the street with her and stood on the corner, watching until she reached Bartow Tower.

Curtis, another member of the building's staff, was on duty when Kasey pushed through the lobby doors.

"Hi there, Ms. Halliday—hey, what happened to you?"

In the light of the lobby, she could see the damage her fall had done, not only torn stockings and scratched shoes but a black sooty stain across her skirt. Her hands were dirty and she imagined her face was, too.

"Nothing serious. I was dodging a speeding car and tripped on the curb."

"I bet it was a taxi. Those damn drivers—pardon me, Ms. Halliday—but those darned drivers pay no attention to the law. Why, one almost took me out over on Broadway last week. Didn't even slow down."

Kasey didn't bother to tell him that his suspicions about the taxi were wrong. Besides, she didn't care about the kind of car, only that she wasn't dead— thanks to Judy's warning.

Curtis, even more solicitous than Tim, walked to the elevator beside Kasey. "Well, I guarantee you'll get safely to your apartment. The elevators are in tip-top condition."

Curtis pushed the button for her. "Almost a week with no problems. Keep your fingers crossed our luck will hold a little while longer."

"At least until I get to my floor. I couldn't handle another calamity tonight." Kasey got on the elevator, and the door closed on Curtis's wide, reassuring smile. She leaned back, feeling drained, now that the adrenaline rush was over. She longed for Will and the comfort of his arms.

As the elevator came to a stop on the nineteenth floor, Kasey's pulse began to beat more quickly. Would Will be there, waiting for her? She stepped out of the elevator into an empty hallway. A little disappointed, she consoled herself with the fact that she'd have a chance to change clothes before rushing to Will.

She crossed to her apartment and stopped, a frown creasing her forehead. There was a florist box at her door. She picked it up curiously, with a glance toward Will's apartment, and went inside.

She opened the card first, setting the box on the living-room table.

Something came up, and I have to cancel our date tonight. Please accept this flower, which is unique and exotic but can't compare with you. Tomorrow night will be special. That's a promise.

Will

Kasey sighed in disappointment, dropped into a chair and opened the box. Inside was an orchid unlike anything she'd ever seen, so deep purple that it was almost black, with a soft yellow throat. It was surrounded by rare and unusual greenery. Kasey lifted the bouquet from the tissue and, handling it carefully, went into the kitchen where she filled a vase and arranged the orchid in it.

His gift was beautiful; there was no doubt about that. But it didn't keep Kasey from feeling upset. She'd desperately wanted to see Will. She tried to think sensibly, telling herself that she should look forward to a long shower and a good night's rest.

Kasey poured herself a glass of wine, took off her scratched shoes and what was left of her stockings and went out onto the balcony, carrying the vase. A slight breeze cooled the hot night, and she could almost imagine a tang of autumn in the air. Summer would soon be ending and somehow that thought was bittersweet.

She walked to the edge of her balcony that joined with Will's and looked over the low railing. She wasn't being nosy, Kasey told herself, she was just interested in what he was doing. Was he at home behind the closed doors? Or had he gone out?

"It's none of your business," she said out loud, chiding herself. Will had a right to a life. He'd lived a lot of years before meeting Kasey, and there was no reason for her to think that everything should stop just because she was a part of his life now.

Of course, she thought, sipping her wine, everything in *her* life seemed to have stopped since he'd come into it. And, dammit, she wanted to know what was going on in his.

She leaned over a little, resting her hand on the railing, peering over at his balcony once more. There was a faint light in his living room. Maybe she'd give him a call just to tell him good-night. Then Kasey realized she didn't even know his phone number. And knowing Will, he was probably unlisted. Besides, he obviously didn't want to be disturbed, and she should respect his privacy.

But it was hard as hell not to be curious.

As she sipped her wine, Kasey drank in the heady scent of the exotic orchid. She'd never experienced anything like the subtle and sensuous aroma of the flower. It was certainly like Will to have found such an unusual gift for her. That gesture touched Kasey. Of course, Judy would see something malicious about that, too. At best, she would call Kasey a romantic fool. Well, she was in love with Will, and if that made her a fool, she didn't care.

As she gazed out over the city lights, her earlier conversation with Judy replayed in her head. Judy had insisted that Will was the catalyst for all the unusual incidents that had plagued her recently. And if Judy heard about the car, she'd probably blame him for that, too.

"It was an accident," Kasey said softly. "Everyone thinks so, and I do, too," she reassured herself.

But Judy's contention that Will had taken advantage of Kasey's vulnerability was eerily close to the truth. She'd remembered the first time they made love—right after the subway incident. But she'd forgotten, or buried somewhere in her psyche, their first kiss. Now she remembered clearly what had happened that night. Will had appeared out of the darkness near Walk-by-Windows. She'd been frightened, and he'd been there for her, protective and caring. Powerfully drawn to him, Kasey had opened herself to him.

"It doesn't mean a thing," she lectured herself. Kasey had been as eager for their kiss—and for their love-making—as Will.

Then why the hell did dark doubts keep hounding her? Kasey drained her wine and went inside. A cool shower, a good night's sleep, and she'd be back to normal. Dark thoughts weren't her style, and she didn't like this brooding side of herself.

She turned off the lights and headed for her bedroom, still pursued by doubts she couldn't shake. Damn, why was Will so secretive? She could understand his running from the television crew in front of Bartow. Lots of people shied away from cameras; there was nothing unusual about that. But he avoided her questions, too, by changing the subject, distracting her, kissing her. And then he'd make love to her.

What about his obsession with the night, his unwillingness to go out into the daylight? Only once had he gone out during the day; that one time when she'd talked him into the picnic in the park. Then suddenly, another almost forgotten image flickered in her memory: the man in the park who'd waved at Will!

She hadn't thought about it again, but now it all came back to her. Will had denied knowing the man. Vehemently. But since then, they hadn't gone out during the day.

Kasey slipped off her clothes and got into bed. Her thoughts were not the exciting ones of the past two days. Now she was haunted by Judy's warnings. The longer she knew Will, the less she seemed to know about him.

She turned out the lights, determined that was going to change. Tomorrow night, she would insist that they talk. She'd been kept in the dark too long.

BY THE NEXT NIGHT, her need to see Will overshadowed all her doubts. Kasey decided to get off early and surprise him. To achieve her plan, she had to bribe Mack into staying late and closing the restaurant, avoid Judy through most of the evening and work like a whirlwind to get eight hours' work done in just over six.

At just past ten o'clock she was home, knocking on his door, out of breath but energized with excitement.

No answer.

Undaunted, she knocked again. This time, Will threw open the door, a scowl on his face that was immediately replaced with surprise.

"Kasey—what in the world . . . ?" He looked at his watch with a frown. "What time is it?"

"I'm early," she announced, and when he didn't immediately respond, she experienced a sudden sinking feeling. Maybe he didn't like surprises. "Hey," she added quickly, "I can go away and come back later."

"Not a chance," he said, pulling her inside. "You just caught me by surprise—"

"And you don't like surprises."

"I'm crazy about them—one in particular." He cradled her face in his hands and kissed her thoroughly. "I was just in the middle of something—"

Kasey moved ahead of him down the hall. She could see the light of his computer screen glowing in the living room. "You're working at the computer."

"Nothing important." He crossed to the desk and hit a couple of keys. "And you're the kind of interruption I crave. Come on," he said, returning to Kasey and enfolding her in his arms. "Let's go over to your place and get back into that comfortable bed," he suggested, giving her a little push toward the hall.

Kasey looked up at him beseechingly. "Can't we stay here? I'd like to spend a night in your bed."

"Well—" he looked around at the living-room office "—this is kind of unromantic . . ."

"Not with you here," Kasey said boldly. "I've missed you, Will. And even though I loved the orchid, it didn't quite take your place."

"It's more exotic," he said, kissing her neck.

"Mmm." The touch of his lips at the hollow in her throat caused an involuntary tremor.

"It's much sweeter-smelling."

"Mmm." Kasey felt the smoothness of his face against her neck. "But it's not as beautiful as you clean-shaven."

"Men aren't beautiful," Will reminded her.

"So you say." She pulled away just enough to look up at him. "But you'll never prove it to me," she added, touching his face with her fingers before reaching up to kiss his cheek, and then his mouth, licking him along the line of his bottom lip and tracing his upper lip with her tongue.

Will stood very still as she tasted him thoroughly. Then he said in a near whisper, "You can't imagine how much I like it when you do that."

"Really?" Kasey put her arms around his neck and pressed herself against him as she continued to drink from his soft, tantalizing lips. "You did the same thing to me in the middle of the night. Remember?"

"Yes, I remember."

"And I remember how wonderful it felt." She nibbled at his lower lip. "And I wanted you to know, too."

"Now I do. I've been thinking about this all day," he told her between kisses. "Waiting till midnight when I could see you again, feel you. And then you surprise me by coming home early. Do you realized that gives us almost two extra hours?"

"For what?" she teased.

"For this." He covered her lips with his, drawing them into his mouth, consuming them and her.

When the kiss ended, her head was reeling. "Still want to stay here?" he asked. "Your bed is more comfortable."

"Yours is closer," she reminded him.

"You win." He drew her down the hall into the bedroom. Along the way, they managed to shed their outer clothes, his T-shirt and trousers, her blouse and skirt. By the time they got to the bed, everything else had been peeled off, tossed aside, and they were together, bodies entwined, tasting and touching.

It was both familiar and all new for Kasey. "It's crazy," she said. "I feel as though we've been apart for weeks..."

"Months," he added. "In a way, it's like we've never been together at all. Somehow," he murmured, "I have the feeling it'll always be new and exciting for us, Kasey."

"I know, I—" She couldn't finish the sentence because of what she was feeling. His mouth or his hands seemed to touch every part of her body. Her lips, her breasts, the moistness between her legs. He excited her everywhere, turned her on fire for him.

"Oh," she managed to moan, "that feels so good. Don't stop. Please, Will—"

He continued to explore her thoroughly until she was weak with longing. "You give me such pleasure," she whispered at last. "I want to do the same for you."

"I'm yours," he replied. "Totally. Completely."

Her head still swimming with desire, she propped up on one elbow and looked at Will, stretched out naked on the bed beside her.

"Do whatever you want with me," he said with a wicked grin.

"I intend to," she told him. "It's time for me to take advantage of you." Her voice was a husky growl. "Starting now."

She leaned over, kissing his mouth and letting her lips enjoy his smooth cheek, his chin, his neck. She moved along the line of his collarbone, used her tongue to taste and tempt his small, hard nipples. He groaned a little, and she smiled. His abdomen was flat and she skimmed little kisses across the warm flesh of it, circled his belly button with her tongue and nibbled on the edge of his hipbone.

Slowly, languidly, she let her hands glide through the fine dark hair around his erection and then held him with her fingers, stroked him, caressed him.

Will let out his breath in a long passionate sigh. Kasey had the power to drive him wild. Then she took him in her hot, slick mouth and he felt such a jolt of pure ecstasy that he gasped. Lights danced inside his head, a myriad of colors, brighter than any rainbow. He felt as though he might explode into a thousand pieces.

Quickly, almost roughly, Will pulled her to him. She slid down on his erection, one pleasurable inch at a time until he filled her completely. They moved together, slowly at first, and then more passionately. His eyes locked onto her face, her beautiful, glowing face, alight with desire and excitement. He couldn't hold back, couldn't stop the spiraling spasms that rocked him with erotic need.

When their release came, it was prolonged and powerful.

He drew her down into his arms and held on tightly, never wanting to let her go, afraid—suddenly—that if he told her the truth, he might lose her. But if he kept living this lie, he would lose her for sure.

KASEY WOKE UP and looked at the luminous dial on the bedside clock—1:00 a.m. She stretched a little and squinted in the half darkness at Will, who slept fretfully, his face creased in a frown. She touched his forehead lightly with the tips of her fingers, smoothing his skin. He moaned softly and turned over.

For a moment, Kasey was tempted to wake him up with a few carefully placed kisses. But something stopped her. He seemed uneasy and in need of sleep. She decided not to disturb him. Whatever was on his mind they could talk about later. They seriously needed to talk, but once again, she'd got sidetracked by the magic of their lovemaking.

Kasey slipped out of bed, picked up his T-shirt from the hall and pulled it over her head. She was very thirsty and a little hungry. Should she raid his refrigerator? Why not? Will made himself at home in her place.

She turned on the kitchen light, found a glass and filled it with water from the tap. Draining it, she opened the refrigerator and surveyed the contents. Milk. Eggs. And a variety of white cartons. She pulled one out and looked inside. Chicken, snowpeas and sprouts. She put it back and didn't bother to check out the others, pretty sure they all contained the same thing: leftovers from Chinese take-out. Her appetite suddenly gone, Kasey filled her glass again and wandered into the living room.

A low lamp glowed on the desk next to the computer. This area was all Will's, and she looked around it curiously. Books were stacked everywhere, arranged as haphazardly as they had been the first day she'd seen the apartment. But this time she had a chance to look at them.

"I'm not snooping," Kasey muttered, "just looking at his books." She glanced at a stack next to the computer, surprised by the titles: *Studies in Erotomania*,

Delusions and Eroticism. The Obsessive Personality. The Psychology of a Stalker.

A prickle of uneasiness crept along her spine as she read the ominous titles again. Why did Will have these books? To learn about someone's warped personality—or his own? As she stood in the shadowy light, shivering involuntarily, Will's words came back to haunt her. "There are lots of crazy people around, Kasey," he'd said. Was he talking about himself? No, Kasey decided. Will certainly wasn't crazy.

But he had a strange choice of reading material.

That was another thing they'd need to talk about, Kasey realized. As she moved away, she bumped into a chair which hit the wobbly desk and sent a pile of letters onto the floor. When Kasey bent down to pick them up, her eyes caught the name and address on the top envelope: William Mastane, 123 Deerfoot Road, Hartville, Connecticut.

Mastane. Something about the name held her interest, skittering around in her head familiarly. She riffled through the other letters, all addressed to the same man, and wondered about the connection between William Mastane and her lover.

Totally puzzled, Kasey turned off the light and noticed that the computer was still on, a bright yellow menu displayed on the monitor. She stood before it for a long time, analyzing her choices. She could walk away, leaving the computer on. Or she could turn it off, hoping he'd saved his last file.

Or she could open one of the files.

Kasey was surprised at her thoughts; it wasn't like her to be suspicious. She turned away quickly so she wouldn't be tempted. Just as quickly, she turned back and before she could stop herself, she hit a key.

A list of files was displayed. She drew a long startled breath as her eyes ran down the choices.

"Act one, scene one, scene two. Act two, scene one . . ." She read them aloud.

Then another voice interrupted hers. It was anything but pleasant.

"What the hell are you doing?"

9

HIS HAND on her shoulder was like a jolt of electricity. Kasey let out a stifled scream and turned, looking into Will's angry face.

"I asked you a question, Kasey." There was fury in his eyes. He had pulled on a pair of trousers, but his chest was bare. He looked big and powerful. And dangerous—with his anger directed at her. "What are you doing?" he repeated.

"Nothing, I—"

"Do you call getting into my computer files nothing?"

"I didn't get into your files," she said defensively. "When I couldn't sleep, I came in here. The light was on, I saw the books—"

"I'm not talking about the books, Kasey."

"Well, I am!" she retorted. "When you find out that the man who has become your lover collects books about erotomania, you begin to wonder what else is going on. Especially when you're not exactly sure what erotomania is," she added.

"The delusional attachment to an object of love," Will said. "That's the textbook answer, anyway."

"I guess I wanted to know why you were reading about that. Maybe I thought I'd find the answer in your files."

Will leaned back against the desk, his arms crossed over his muscled chest, staring at her steadily.

Kasey felt herself backing down. "I'm sorry," she told him. "I apologize for my curiosity. It was wrong of me to act on it, but why wouldn't I, when I innocently walk in here and see things that seem to belong to another person? The books and then your computer files—"

"How did that strike you, Kasey?"

She realized that she wasn't quite sure, but she bristled at the condescending way he'd asked the question. "It *struck me* that someone had written a play. You, I guess."

"Well, you're right. I wrote it, but it's not actually a play." He crossed in front of her, reached into a drawer and handed her a document in a green plastic binder.

She turned to the first page and read the title aloud. "'The Hemlock Tree,' a television script by William Mastane." She looked down at the mail on his desk and then across at him. "Eastman. Mastane. It's an anagram, the same letters rearranged. You're William Mastane!"

"Yes," he said simply.

Kasey's mind whirled, and there was a sick feeling in the pit of her stomach. What the hell was going on? A terrible sense of dread encompassed her.

"You lied to me about your name. Why?" She wrapped her arms around the script and clutched it to her chest. "And you didn't even tell me what you did for a living. In fact, you lied about that, too. Taxi driver, construction worker . . . Did you lie about everything, Will?"

"Writers take all kinds of second jobs. That was no lie."

"But your name?"

"It seemed best for me not to use my real name."

She dropped the script onto the desk as if it were suddenly red-hot.

He watched that move without comment.

Why did you lie to *me?*" she asked. "I thought we had something special. I thought we trusted each other. I even thought—"

"Go on." He didn't move a muscle as he watched her. "You thought . . ."

Kasey met his hard gaze evenly. "I thought we were falling in love." She gave a bitter laugh. "I was going to tell you. Tonight. That I loved you. I guess you think I'm a real fool."

"Not you, Kasey. Never you. You're a woman who says what she believes and feels. Up to now, I haven't been able to do that."

"So instead you lie! Lie to me and then make love?" She moved across the room, as far away from the desk and Will as she could get. She wanted to leave, to get away from him completely, but not until she found out why he'd made a fool of her.

"Making love wasn't a lie, Kasey. That's the only true part of this whole mess. I wish I could explain what's going on, but I can't."

"What do you mean by that? Is there something else?"

"Not that you need to know about." His face was set in stubborn lines. "I care for you. I'll take care of you. Isn't that enough?"

"No, it isn't! I didn't ask you to take care of me. I can take care of myself." Her shock and hurt were swiftly being replaced by a burgeoning wave of anger. "What I wanted was honesty and respect, and I'm getting neither from you. Why can't you tell me what's going on?"

"Because I don't want to involve you. I have to handle this myself. I have to get her—get it—out of my life."

Kasey drew in a breath. "Did you say get *her* out of your life? Who do you mean, your wife? Did you lie to me about her, too?"

"No, I didn't. Look, Kasey," he said, moving closer to her, for the first time, "that was a slip, and I think you overreacted to it. If you'll just be calm—"

"Don't talk to me like that, Will. Or William," she amended bitterly. "And don't expect me to be calm when I've just found out that every word you've said to me is a lie."

"That's not true, Kasey."

"Then what *is* true? Why won't you tell me why the hell you're going through this stupid charade, lying to me, to my friends, even to the apartment staff? What's the matter with you? Tell me what it's all about!" she demanded, feeling as if her head were about to explode.

Her angry glare was met by his own closed gaze. "I told you once, Kasey. I'm not going to involve you in something that I need to handle myself, alone. If you'll just trust me for a while—"

Kasey couldn't believe her ears. "Trust you? Trust you! I'd just as soon trust a roomful of rattlesnakes."

"Kasey—"

"No more," she shouted with a sob as she pushed past him and ran down the hall. After gathering her clothes and handbag, she headed for the front door.

Will grabbed her arm from behind, but she pulled angrily away. "Don't touch me," she warned, "or I'll scream the building down. I'm going home. Alone. And I'm going to count my blessings that I found out about you when I did."

"I won't let you go, Kasey," Will said, moving around in front of her and blocking her way. "Not until we talk about this. If you'll just calm down—"

She looked up at him, her face white with rage. "I'll calm down all right—when you tell me who you are, why you're playing these damned games with me and with everyone else." She took a deep breath. "Until then, get out of my way!"

Will swore bitterly under his breath as Kasey pushed by him.

She was out the door, fumbling with her keys. Not realizing that she wore nothing but his T-shirt, she charged to her apartment, unlocked it and pushed her way inside. She slammed the door behind her and leaned back against it, her eyes closed, breathing deeply. Then she turned the bolt and put on the chain, as if by doing that she would keep Will out of her life.

"Fool, fool, fool," she muttered as she stalked down the hall to her living room, ignoring the pounding on her door. She didn't give a damn if Will knocked all night long. Kasey had always been slow to anger, but when the anger hit, she exploded like a volcano. The eruption had begun, and she had a feeling there was more to come.

By the time she reached her bedroom, the pounding had stopped, but now the phone by her bed was ringing. She couldn't listen to *that* all night, Kasey decided as she picked up the receiver and tossed it on the bed. So much for Will. Let him talk to himself for a while. All she wanted was a cool, clean shower to wash away every trace of him that lingered on her skin.

She went into the bathroom and had pulled Will's T-shirt halfway off, when she saw the writing on the mirror. It jumped out at her in blood-red letters:

DIE BITCH

She couldn't stop screaming. The sound of her voice reverberated around the room and echoed in her ears. When she finally stopped, her breath came in rapid gasps. She held on to the basin with both hands, steadying her shaking legs, fighting for control until her heart began to beat less wildly.

Then the question pounded in her head. "No," she cried. "Not Will! It can't be him." The trembling began again and this time she couldn't control it. She collapsed onto the side of the tub. "It's not possible," she whispered.

But if not Will, then who? Someone had got into her apartment, invaded her privacy and threatened her, and all she could do was shake.

"No, dammit," she said aloud. "I won't be intimidated! Whatever is going on, I'm getting to the bottom of it."

She rushed into the bedroom, pulled on her jeans and stuck her feet into her sneakers. That's when it hit her.

She knew how the intruder had got in. She'd left the balcony doors open!

She charged angrily into the living room and saw that she was right. The doors were unlocked. Cursing herself for her carelessness, Kasey pulled them together and fastened the latch. That's when she heard the noise—from the balcony. Someone was out there!

She didn't stop to wonder who it was. This time, she wasn't going to take any chances. She dashed into the kitchen, grabbed the wall phone and punched in 911.

But when she put the phone to her ear, there was no ringing. She hung up and tried again. No dial tone. No sound at all. The phone was dead!

She slammed down the receiver, and as she caught her breath, trying to think, she heard the noise again, louder this time. Suddenly, she saw a shape on the terrace, a dark menacing shadow, beating against the door.

Then she remembered. The bedroom phone was off the hook! She ran across the living room, heading toward the hall just as the figure threw his body against the balcony doors. With the splintering of wood and breaking of glass, he hurled himself into her apartment.

Kasey froze for an instant and then turned to run, but he was faster. He grabbed her around the waist and held her high, lifting her feet from the floor. Impotently, she kicked out at him, struggling wildly in his arms.

"Kasey, stop it. It's me, Will."

"I know that," she cried, "and I'm calling the police."

"No, you're not. Not yet, anyway." He held her fast, and Kasey knew she wasn't going to get away.

"Then I'll scream. If you don't let me go, I'll scream and—"

"You screamed before, Kasey. That's why I broke in. I thought you were in trouble—"

"I was—I am! And you're the cause of it."

"There's no one else in here?" he asked.

She shook her head. The impulse to scream had passed.

He carried her to the sofa and sat down beside her, his arms tight around her. His mouth was close to her ear, and she could feel the heat and power emanating from his body. "Listen to me, Kasey. I'm not going to hurt you, but you have to tell me what happened. Who frightened you?"

She fell back against the sofa. "No one. There's a death threat on my mirror, that's all."

"What?"

"Yes, I don't know who did it, but I know that I'm scared, and I'm tired of being scared. I'm calling the police—"

Will was up in a heartbeat, heading for the bathroom. He reappeared only seconds later, swearing under his breath, and sat down beside her. "I never meant for this to happen, Kasey. Not for you to be threatened, too . . ."

"Threatened *too?*" she cried, her anger returning. "It's time to stop playing games with me, Will. Now you *have* to tell me what the hell's going on."

Will's face was drawn and white, and there was a deep dark look in his eyes.

"I'm not sure where to begin," he said slowly.

"At the beginning," Kasey demanded.

The time had come; Will knew that. He put his head in his hands and was quiet for a long time, thinking, or trying to. It wasn't easy for him to tell Kasey, to make enough sense out of what was happening that she would understand. "This is going to sound crazy," he said finally, looking over at her. She seemed so young and vulnerable, dressed in his oversize T-shirt, her blue eyes filled with pain.

"I want to know," she persisted.

"Okay," he said. "I'm being stalked."

He watched her reaction. Her face was tight with tension, the pain still in her eyes. What had he done to her?

"It started months ago—"

"Why didn't you tell me?" she asked.

"I didn't want any harm to come to you."

The look she gave him was one of total disbelief.

"All right. I know now that I was wrong, Kasey. I just never expected her to go after you."

Kasey sank back on the sofa.

"Do you still want to hear this?"

"Why not?" she said with a shrug.

"A few months ago, I got a letter from a woman who claimed to be a big fan. I answered the letter, which I always try to do. In this case, that was a big mistake."

Kasey made a disdainful noise.

"I was working at my place in Connecticut, a little cottage back in the woods. She began to call me, telling me how much she loved my work. Then how much she loved *me*. The calls got weirder. We were meant to be together, according to her, and nothing I said could convince her that I wasn't interested."

"Erotomania," Kasey said, almost to herself.

"Yes. An obsession. Somehow, she'd learned what she wanted to know, that I wasn't married and there was no woman in my life. Except her, of course," he commented wryly. "I thought getting an unlisted number would put an end to it, but the calls kept coming. I have no idea how she got my number, but she did. That's when I got really angry."

"About time, I'd say," Kasey commented bitterly.

"I know, Kasey, but I didn't realize how deeply disturbed she was. I tried to handle her with understanding at first."

"What happened when you got angry?"

"She decided I was committed to her."

Kasey frowned at him.

"I know, it's crazy. But that's often how it happens. I've actually read those books you discovered in my office. People with this disease often take rejections as 'tests of loyalty.' No matter what I said, she still believed that I was involved in her life in an intimate, fateful way. She even thought one of my TV movies was based on her life, which proved we were soul mates."

"My God," Kasey said.

"It gets worse. When I didn't respond to her letters or the notes in my car and under my front door, she threatened me."

Kasey gave a shiver and wrapped her arms around herself. "What do you mean?"

"They were death threats, actually. If she couldn't have me, no one would. I called the police, but there

wasn't much they could do. Doubled patrols, added
shifts in my area, but they never even saw the woman.
Neither did I. She was playing games with all of us. Finally, the cops suggested I move out of the house and
lose myself in a big city for a while—"

"That's when you came to New York."

"No, not then. I was damned if I would be driven
away from my own home. But that was before she
broke into the house when I was out. Trashed the computer, destroyed scripts, burned family photos, slashed
furniture. God, it was a mess. And she left a note, of
course. She wrote that she wanted to become the most
important person in my life. She was succeeding in that
wish," he said bitterly.

"You finally got out," Kasey said.

Will looked over at her, trying to figure out what she
thought of his indecisiveness. Not much, he decided.
"My agent was the catalyst for my leaving, I'll admit.
He got together with the network producer and put
pressure on me to get the special project I was working
on finished. I wasn't having much luck in Connecticut
so I agreed to go into hiding until it was completed.
They insisted that I keep my real identity a secret."

"Even from the woman you were sleeping with?"
Kasey's voice was bitter.

Will got up from the sofa and walked to the middle
of the room before turning to look at Kasey. "You want
to know something? The first day I met you, I wondered if you could be the stalker."

"That's why you were so wary! And I thought you
were just being arrogant."

"I couldn't trust anyone at that point. Then when we ended up in the basement—"

"You thought I'd set that up."

"Until I realized how scared you were of me."

Kasey started to laugh. Her shoulders shook, and she covered her face with her hands. Will sat beside her and pulled her hands away. "Are you getting hysterical, Kasey?"

"No. Yes. I don't know! You see, I thought *I* was being stalked."

"Not by me?"

"No, by the guy I told you about, the one who used to work at the restaurant. Oh, God." Her eyes widened in fear. "It was her, wasn't it? She's responsible for all the weird things that have been happening lately. And now she's after me!"

Will's lips tightened. "Yes, I'm afraid so." He watched her face as that information sank in.

"When we came back from the park . . . The TV cameras . . . She saw you."

Will nodded. "I think she saw both of us. Hell, Kasey, I thought I could protect you better if you knew nothing about her."

Kasey let out a deep, disbelieving sigh.

"Maybe I was wrong—"

"Maybe?"

"Kasey, we don't know what would have happened if you'd known about her. Sometimes a little knowledge can cause big trouble."

"Isn't this big trouble?" she asked.

"You're right," he said, reaching out and touching her arm. "We're both in trouble, and it's my fault. I didn't mean for this to happen. I hope you understand that."

Kasey stood up and pushed her tangled hair away from her face. "You lied to me and put me in danger. That's not easy to understand, especially when I . . . I care about you."

"I care about you, too, Kasey. We can get past this. I know we can."

He reached for her again, but this time Kasey brushed his hand aside. When she spoke, her words lacked emotion. "I'm not sure about that, Will, but I'm certain of one thing. We have to call the police and tell them everything that's happened."

FROM EXPERIENCE, Will didn't expect much help from the police. He told Kasey that, but she insisted on calling. What else could they do?

Two uniformed officers arrived half an hour later and took what seemed to Will to be cursory notes. The woman, Officer Gwen Hererra, was just slightly less disinterested than her partner, Ted Delansky, an older man with graying red hair and mustache, who was barely able to conceal a yawn.

"So you moved down here from Connecticut knowing some woman was stalking you?" Delansky asked.

"I moved here *because* she was stalking me," Will corrected. "I thought that I'd eluded her."

"And now you think she's found you and is harassing Ms. Halliday, too."

"It seems obvious, Officer Delansky," Will answered, "that there's a pattern here."

"Not to me, Mr. Mastane," Delansky stated emphatically.

Officer Hererra explained for her partner. "We have no evidence that the threat on Ms. Halliday's mirror has anything to do with you, Mr. Mastane. It could be totally unrelated. You haven't seen the woman since you moved here."

"Correction, again," Will said. "To my knowledge, I've *never* seen the woman."

"Then we have no evidence," Delansky said, snapping his notebook shut.

Kasey looked hopelessly at Will, who shrugged. He'd known this was coming, and he wasn't surprised.

"We'll run a check on this Carl Dandridge whom you said threatened you," Hererra said. "Is there anyone else who may have it in for you, Ms. Halliday?"

"No. Absolutely not." Kasey caught herself. "Except for the redheaded woman—"

Will noticed that Delansky stopped midyawn and looked interested. "Tell me about her."

"I don't know anything about her, really. She didn't actually threaten me. But she did cause a scene in the restaurant."

Will shook his head hopelessly as the officers glanced at each other with skepticism. They weren't buying the redheaded woman story, either.

"It's not really much to go on," Hererra said softly. "And I imagine people have caused scenes in the restaurant before, haven't they?" she asked Kasey.

"Well, yes, of course. But this was different. Somehow."

Will felt sorry for Kasey. She'd put her hopes in the police, and, frankly, she didn't have much to give them. That was his fault, too, of course. It seemed as if he'd done nothing but make wrong decisions ever since this nightmare began. Now his decisions had affected Kasey.

"Like I said, we don't have a lot to go on," Hererra told them. "There are probably a million redheads in this city."

"That's not all," Kasey said. "There was an incident at the subway. Someone pushed me—"

"Did you see the person?" Hererra asked. Delansky didn't even appear to be listening at this point.

Kasey shook her head.

"Well, it was probably an accident. Those platforms get very crowded," Hererra said.

Kasey felt her shoulders sag. "Well, I—wait a minute, there's one more thing. I just remembered. The car!"

"What car?" Will asked.

"The one that almost hit me. A dark car, no lights, whizzing around the corner."

"Why didn't you tell me about that?" Will scolded.

"You weren't around. Besides, everyone kept saying it was an accident, reminding me that it's hard to go out and not be run over in New York."

"They're right," Hererra agreed. "We deal with hit-and-run cases all the time. Especially—"

Delansky interrupted his partner. "Let's forget about all the accidents and move on. How did the alleged perpetrator gain entrance to your apartment? Have you given your keys to anyone?"

"No, I haven't," Kasey answered. "The super has a set to all the apartments."

"We'll check him out," Delansky said.

"It's really not necessary," Kasey replied.

Will could see that she was getting defensive, and he applauded her silently.

"I'm sure the stalker got in through the doors on my balcony. I must have left them unlocked. When I came home, they were open."

"Well, it's hard to tell much about them now, isn't it?" Delansky asked with a glance at the shattered doorframe and broken glass. "Mr. Mastane really did a job on them."

"I had no choice," Will defended. "I heard her scream. I thought she was in danger."

"So you crossed over from your balcony and broke the doors in. Just as you could have come across earlier and written the message on Ms. Halliday's mirror," Delansky commented.

"But he didn't!" Kasey retorted.

"Who lives on the other side?"

"Mrs. Janek. She's wheelchair-bound," Kasey answered.

"That brings us back to you," Delansky said, looking at Will.

"Oh, please!" Kasey said irritably.

Will sensed Kasey's frustration and spoke for her. "The bottom line is that I'm being stalked—and Ms. Halliday's been threatened. And not by me," he added emphatically.

"We'll check it out," Delansky said. "If someone wrote those words on the mirror, she—or he—could have gotten in anywhere on this floor. It could be any one of your neighbors or someone entering through their apartments." Delansky put away his notebook, but Will noticed he hadn't written in it since he'd concluded there was no evidence.

"And if you were stalked," Delansky said to Will, "the Connecticut police will give us that information."

"They don't have anything more than I've told you," Will said scornfully. With that, the two officers shot each other a final look, and as if on signal, got up to go.

"Oh, Mr. Mastane, I wanted to say—"

"Yes, Officer Hererra?"

"I really enjoyed your television series last season. 'The Lawson Family Diaries' was one of my favorites."

"Thanks," Will replied curtly. He'd hoped to hear something about the case, something that mattered.

"I don't remember him in 'Diaries,'" Delansky said as he walked toward the door with his partner.

"He wasn't in it. He wrote it," Hererra replied.

The police officers left, leaving Will and Kasey sitting in the living room, facing each other.

"I didn't realize you were famous." Kasey's tone wasn't pleasant or even interested. She was angry, Will realized, with the police and probably with him, too.

"I'm not famous," he responded.

She ignored his disclaimer and went on. "They didn't believe us. Did you hear what he said? *If* I were harassed. *If* you were stalked."

"They'll find out that we're not lying. I'm just afraid they won't get the connection. And I know there is one."

"Then why didn't you think of it sooner?" she snapped. "Didn't it dawn on you when I got pushed in front of the subway train that this crazy woman might be behind it?"

Will tried to keep his cool. In a way, she was right, but it didn't seem as if she was ever going to understand what he'd been through. "It didn't occur to me, Kasey. I'd been in New York for some time with no contact from her. It's not her style to wait. If she'd been around, I'd have known."

"But she was around," Kasey retorted. "She could have been driving the car that almost hit me that night. Where were you, anyway?"

"I drove to Connecticut to talk to the police, hoping they had some new information. But they didn't. No surprise." He ran his fingers through his tousled hair. "But unlike the New York police, at least they believe she exists. Unfortunately, I don't know much more except that this type of person is never predictable." He stood up and started pacing again.

He reminded Kasey of a caged animal, just as he had the first day she saw him.

"Maybe that unpredictability is what kept me from telling you everything. I made a choice. We may never know whether it was the right one or not."

She considered that. "When I think of the times I defended you to Judy, swore you weren't hiding anything—"

"If I had told you, what would you have done?" he asked.

"I would have understood!" She stood up, too, facing him. "I would have kept your secret. You didn't have the guts to trust me, Will. Now it's all come back to haunt us."

"This is all about hindsight, Kasey. You think you would have understood? If I'd told you in the beginning that a crazy woman was after me, you'd have run, not walked, to the nearest door. Hell, I tried to warn you a hundred ways. I tried to tell you to back off—"

"And I kept right on coming, didn't I?" she asked. "Because I couldn't help myself, Will. I cared too much." The words were wrenched from her.

He quickly moved to her side and grabbed her by the shoulders. "And so did I. I cared too much to—" There was a knock on the door. "Who the hell is that?"

Kasey started toward the hall, but he stopped her. "Let me get it."

She stepped aside and let him pass, aware that for now, at least, she was glad he was with her. Whoever was at the door, she didn't want to deal with it. She went back and collapsed on the sofa, staring at the broken doors, wondering what she was going to tell Tim about the commotion. Then she remembered. The police would tell him. In fact, they probably already had.

Will came back into the room. "The cops have completed their so-called investigation. Want to hear the results?"

"Why not."

"The couple across the hall was home all evening watching TV. They saw nothing. Heard nothing. Your friend Glenna was entertaining a guy. She saw nothing. Heard nothing. Same for everyone else on the floor. Your Mrs. Janek—"

"She's not my Mrs. Janek," Kasey said.

"Well, she was asleep. There's an empty apartment on this floor. They'll check with the super to see if he gave out the keys to anyone."

"That's it? That's all they're doing?"

"It's more than I expected, to tell you the truth," Will replied. "Oh, they'll check out the guy from your restaurant and follow up in Connecticut, so they say. Basically, they're writing it off as a prank."

"What a mess," Kasey said. "After all that's happened, they think someone's playing a joke on me."

"Well, Delansky probably thinks it's me. Or that Spiderman climbed down from the penthouse. Hell, Kasey, we're on our own. Why don't you get your things and come to my place for the night? We still need to talk."

Kasey sat up straight. "No way. Forget it."

"Kasey, after all that's happened, I'm not going to let any harm come to you. Ever. And you can't sleep here," he told her. "Not with broken doors. I'll call the super and ask him to get someone over here to repair it tomorrow while you're at work."

"Meanwhile, I'll go to Glenna's—"

"She has company, remember? Come to my place, Kasey. It's the only sensible thing to do. Unless you share Delansky's view. Unless you're afraid of me."

She met his eyes evenly. "No, Will, I'm not afraid of you, but I'm still angry. I need some time—and space."

"Don't worry. I'll sleep on the sofa. Come on, Kasey," he urged more gently. "You're exhausted."

AFTER AN ARGUMENT about who would sleep where, Kasey gave in and took the bed. It was a strange experience, she mused, being alone in Will's bed when only hours before they'd shared it, wrapped in each other's arms.

Only then she hadn't known who he was. Now she did, and according to Officer Hererra, he was something of a celebrity. Kasey wasn't impressed. Famous writer or not, how dare he play games with her that way?

Maybe he was just trying to protect her, Kasey's subconscious whispered. Maybe he didn't trust easily. Kasey turned restlessly, from one side to the other. Obviously, trust wasn't a problem with her; she trusted far *too* easily. But if she hadn't been trusting, she never would have met him! It was so complex. Everything in her life seemed contradictory and confusing.

She couldn't sleep. After half an hour, she sat up on the edge of the bed. It was pointless to lie here fretting, she decided. She got up. Opening the door, she was surprised to see a light from the living room.

Will was sitting at his computer, deep in thought.

"I couldn't sleep, either," she said softly to avoid startling him.

He turned to look at her. His face was tired, haggard. "Would you like a drink? Wine?"

"No, nothing." She wandered to the balcony doors. "So many people in this city... We'll never find her, the police will never find her."

His voice was grim. "But she can find us. And she already has."

"Is—erotomania—serious?" Kasey sat on the arm of the sofa. "You've read all about it. Is it a disease that...I mean, do you think she'd...kill someone?"

Will pushed away from his desk and leaned back in his chair. He clasped his hands behind his neck and stared at the ceiling thoughtfully. "I really can't answer that, Kasey, based on my reading."

"But you have an opinion." She was a little afraid of the response.

"Most of these people are bright, functioning individuals who hold down a job and appear completely normal," he told her.

"Except toward the person they're stalking."

"Right. Then they can lose sight of reality. I told you that she considered my rejection of her as a test of loyalty. Well, there's more. They sometimes believe that the object of their love is sending secret signals."

"Like appearing on TV?"

"Yes. And even worse, I was wearing a crazy looking T-shirt that couldn't be missed. She might have seen me wearing it before. It was a mistake to wear it, but I hadn't planned to be on television. She probably took that as a sign of my hidden affection. And seeing you with me—"

"Now she hates me because I've taken you away from her. And she could try to harm me, couldn't she?"

"She's not going to," he said quickly. "I meant what I said before, Kasey, I won't let that happen. You mean too much to me." He put his hand on her knee. Her robe had fallen open, and he stroked the filmy material of her nightgown. "You know how I feel about you—"

"Don't, Will," she said, moving away.

"Can't we talk about this, about us?"

Kasey stood up. "Not now. I can't talk about us yet."

"Then tomorrow. When you get back from work."

"All right. I promise. Now I'm going to try to sleep." She walked away and then turned back, pausing at the door. "Will, the man who waved at you in the park—you knew him, didn't you?"

"Yeah, I worked with him on a TV special."

And you lied again, Kasey thought. She gave him a sad little smile. "See you in the morning, Will."

10

WILL AWOKE before Kasey and decided to let her sleep. He knew she was exhausted. He hadn't slept that well, either, having spent most of the night thinking about how he had botched up his life. There had to be a way to make everything right again.

He went into the kitchen and made a pot of coffee. When he heard Kasey stir, he decided to take a stab at cooking breakfast. He opened the refrigerator door and surveyed the possibilities. Eggs. That was about it. He took them out and looked in the freezer to discover a can of orange juice and a package of English muffins. He dropped the can of juice into a bowl, filled it with hot water, broke off a couple of muffins and put them in the microwave to defrost.

He was a pretty good cook when he took the time, but there had been too many other things on Will's mind this summer. At least he could fix breakfast for Kasey, he decided, as he transferred the muffins to the toaster oven.

"Butter," he said aloud, opening the fridge hopefully. There it was, untouched, still in the store wrapping. He buttered the muffins liberally, put them back in the toaster oven, and by the time Kasey came into the kitchen, her hair damp and her face scrubbed shiny clean, he was making an omelet.

"I hope you'll stay for breakfast. The coffee's ready." He saw her hesitate and urged, "Come on, Kasey, test my culinary skills."

"I didn't know you could cook."

"There's a lot you don't know," he told her.

"*That's* the truth."

Damn. He'd walked right into that one. "A lot of good things, Kasey. Like the summer I spent in France. That's where I learned to make a mean omelet. Try it, won't you?"

"All right," she said as she filled a mug with coffee and leaned against the counter. "So you're a world traveler."

"Not the whole world, but a lot of it. I told you that when we had our picnic in the park."

Another wrong move, he realized when he saw the look on Kasey's face. "Juice?"

Kasey nodded.

Will kept the conversation going as he mixed the juice in a pitcher. "After the sale of my first TV movie, I went to Europe for a while. I was divorced by then and on my own, so I traveled and just hung out with no real agenda. The second script hit and then the third. I took a trip to the Orient. It was a kind of reward for myself."

"None of that sounds like a state secret," Kasey said bitterly. "You could have shared it with me earlier."

"I know, and I'm sorry. I haven't been thinking straight, Kasey." Her face was still wary. He wondered what the hell *she* was thinking.

"What about the other things you told me, about being an only child—" She sounded angry and suspicious.

"All true. My parents are retired and living in Vermont. My ex-wife is in Boston, happily remarried. We got divorced about six years ago when I was twenty-five and still a struggling writer. She wanted me to give up and get what she called a 'real job,' but I was committed to risking it as a writer. She didn't want to struggle with me and I don't blame her. I was still a couple of years away from success—and it might not have come at all. The divorce worked out for both of us."

Kasey started to comment, but he wasn't finished. "If I'd told you more about her and the divorce, we'd have gotten into my writing. From there, it wouldn't have taken you long to ask why I was in New York, hiding out."

Before she could confront him again, Will offered quickly, "How about breakfast outside? There are English muffins in the toaster oven and the orange juice is poured."

When she didn't object, he filled their plates and led the way to the balcony. There was something else he had to say, but it wasn't time yet. He wanted to enjoy breakfast first.

Even this early in the morning, the heat was oppressive. A gray haze hung over the city like a pall. They ate in silence. When they'd finished, Kasey looked across the table at Will. "The omelet was lovely. Thanks."

He nodded.

"It's not a very lovely day, though."

Will took a sip of coffee and put down his cup. "I don't give a damn about the omelet or the weather, Kasey. What I do care about is you. And whether or not you want to hear this, I have to say it. Now."

Before she could reply, he went on. "I've been thinking about it all night." He looked at her steadily. "Kasey Halliday, you're the most important person in my life. I wish to hell I hadn't lied to you. I wish I'd given you a chance to decide for yourself how you felt about the whole scenario. But I didn't and—"

"And if you'd told me, I don't know how I would have felt," she interrupted. "But I've been doing some thinking, too, Will. And I realize that my knowing about the stalker couldn't have stopped her from pushing me at the subway or breaking into my apartment—"

"Maybe not, but there was still no reason for me to lie. I should have protected you. But it's not too late, thank God. I'm going to take care of you from now on." He reached across the table for her hand, and she grasped his tightly. He thought he saw the sheen of tears in her eyes. "What is it, Kasey?"

"Nothing. I mean, I'm usually the one who takes care of people. It's nice to be taken care of for a change."

"Wouldn't it be great to think that we could take care of each other? But that wouldn't be fair." He paused before adding, "I should get out of your life now, and try to draw that crazy witch away from you."

"No," she said quickly. "I don't want you to go."

Will felt great relief wash over him. "I don't want to." He held on to her hand, looking deeply into her eyes.

"Even with all this horror, something magical has happened, Kasey. We've met, and we've—"

"Fallen in love," she said softly. "I'm not afraid to say it, are you?"

"Not at all. I love you, Kasey, with all my heart."

AFTER WORK that night, she shared a taxi with Judy, who insisted on going around the block and pulling up in front of Bartow Tower, where she put a restraining hand on Kasey's arm. "Let me walk in with you."

"Judy, for heaven's sake. I can see Tim from here, and I can certainly walk the twenty feet to the door in safety."

Judy didn't let go. "Listen to me, Kasey. You don't know where this crazy woman will turn up. I think you should come home with me—"

"Hey, ladies, I ain't got all night," the driver said, turning around. "In or out?"

"Out," Kasey said emphatically as she gave Judy a hug and broke away from her grasp. "I'll be fine. Will is waiting for me, and we're going to take care of each other."

"Well, I hope so." She still kept a tenacious hold on Kasey's sleeve.

"Judy—"

"Okay, you're too stubborn for me. You win. I'll call in the morning. Please be careful."

"Are you kidding?" Kasey asked as she handed over her half of the fare. "Caution is my middle name."

She ducked into the building and gave Judy a wave as the taxi pulled away. On his stool, Tim looked up from behind the newspaper. "Am I glad to see you, Ms. Halliday."

Startled, Kasey asked, "Why, is something the matter?"

Tim shook his head. "Nothing serious. It's just your next-door neighbor, Mrs. Janek. She's called down three times tonight asking for you to stop by her apartment."

Kasey groaned inwardly. "What's her problem, Tim?"

"That's just it. She didn't want to tell me. She said it was something only you could help her with." He lowered his voice and blushed as he added, "I have a feeling it's some kind of female thing."

"Damn," Kasey said under her breath. She'd left work a little early so she could indulge herself in a cool, relaxing bath. Will had asked her to go straight to his apartment, but she planned to surprise him, powdered and perfumed, wearing something casual but sexy. Well, she'd just have to take care of Mrs. Janek's problem quickly, before her bath.

"Wonder what it could possibly be," she mumbled.

Tim was there with his own idea. "Actually, I think she heard about your bad experience the other night, and got a little paranoid. She may just need some company."

"Well, only for a few minutes," Kasey decided. "I'm a little paranoid myself, so watch the elevator, and be sure it goes straight to the nineteenth floor. If it stops on the way, sound the alarm and send for the cavalry," Kasey said with a laugh.

As she got in the elevator and pushed number nineteen, she didn't feel all that amused. In fact, she felt edgy and nervous. Will's stalker could be in the building. Kasey had no idea what she looked like. Tall, short, fat, thin? The stalker could stop the elevator on any floor, get on—and Kasey would be virtually helpless.

"I should have taken those karate classes," she said aloud, thinking of the self-defense course Judy and some of the waitresses at work had taken a few months before. She held her breath as the floor numbers flashed before her, sixteen, seventeen, eighteen. She was almost home.

The doors slid open on nineteen and Kasey stepped out and looked both ways, relieved to see the floor was empty. She knocked on Mrs. Janek's door. She'd take care of this quickly, she decided, thinking a little guiltily that she'd promised to check in on the older woman and so far hadn't. Of course, she'd been otherwise occupied with problems of her own, Kasey thought wryly.

She knocked again and then realized that the door was ajar. Tim must have called and told Mrs. Janek that Kasey was on the way. She pushed open the door and stepped inside.

"Mrs. Janek, are you there? It's Kasey."

There was silence in the dark foyer, and suddenly Kasey panicked. Could the stalker have got in somehow? She wasn't going to stay and find out; she was going to get Will!

She turned back toward the hall, heard a noise behind her and tried to move away, but it was too late. She felt a painful blow to her head, and suddenly everything went black.

KASEY CAME TO SLOWLY, her head throbbing. For a brief instant, she felt the pain and forgot the rest. Then she remembered, in horror, that she was in Mrs. Janek's apartment—and so was the stalker!

She opened her eyes slowly, a millimeter at a time. If the stalker was nearby, she didn't want to reveal that she was awake. The light was on now, blinding her. She blinked against its glare. God, her head hurt. She tried to touch the aching spot and realized that she couldn't move her hand. She was bound at the wrists—and ankles—in Mrs. Janek's wheelchair!

Frantically, Kasey squirmed against the ropes, but they didn't budge. Her brain struggled to make sense out of what was going on as her body struggled in the wheelchair. Where was Mrs. Janek? What had happened to the old woman? Had the stalker overpowered her—or killed her?

Kasey shook her head, trying to clear her thoughts, and caused a sharp pain to shoot along her temples. She couldn't hold back an agonizing moan, but in spite of the pain, she forced herself to move her head and look around. The bedroom door was open, and she could see the corner of a bed and next to it, atop a low chest, two wigs on stands. One gray. One red.

A chill of comprehension ran along Kasey's spine, and her heart caught in her throat. She knew the stalker's identity—and she had never been more frightened in her life.

At the height of her panic, a woman emerged from the bedroom, her short hair neither red nor gray, but a dull brown. She was average height and weight. Overall, she was an unremarkable-looking woman. Except for her eyes. Kasey had seen those eyes before.

Kasey exhaled a shaky breath, speaking the woman's name. "Mrs. Janek."

"Yes. And also your redheaded harasser." The woman pulled up a straight chair and sat in the bedroom doorway across from Kasey. Her lips curved in a smile. "Let me introduce myself, Kasey, dear. My name is Abby Dorset, and I'm an actress. A very talented one, as I'm sure you will agree." For those last words, she used the elderly Freya Janek's voice to perfection.

Kasey sat in the wheelchair, staring at the woman, her heart pounding so loudly that she was sure Abby Dorset could hear it. Her mouth was dry, and she didn't think she would be able to speak again. She swallowed hard, and the words came. "You're the woman who's after Will."

"Brava, brava," Abby commented sarcastically. "But I must correct your interpretation. I'm not *after* Will. He and I were meant to be together. It's unfortunate that you chose to come between us."

Kasey's head swam. This was a nightmare come true. She knew the woman seated before her was dangerous, and she didn't want to antagonize her. Yet common sense told Kasey to keep Abby talking, to play for time and pray Will would come after her. She had a feeling Will's stalker would be willing to talk about him and their "relationship."

"What do you want from Will?" she asked cautiously.

"I want him to be mine, you must know that."

"Did you tell him that?"

"I don't have to tell him. He knows. He's known since the moment we met."

Kasey tried not to think about the pounding ache in her head and concentrated on her conversation with Abby. "Where did you meet him?"

"At an audition, where else?" Abby seemed surprised at the question. "I tried out for a role in one of his television movies. They sent me the entire script instead of the sides—the lines I needed to learn. I took that as an omen. When I read the script, I realized that it was the story of my life. I knew the part would be mine."

"Did you tell him?"

"Tell Will? I didn't have to. He understood. From the moment I walked into the audition studio, there was something between us, something beautiful. It was the closest thing to magic that I've ever known. It was as if we could read each other's souls. And of course, he wanted me in the role. He wrote it for me, in fact."

"Did you get the part?"

"No, I didn't."

From the look on Abby's face, Kasey feared that she'd gone too far. Then, to her surprise, Abby smiled. "It wasn't Will's fault. I could tell from the way he looked at me, from the way he said, 'Thank you, Ms. Dorset, we'll be in touch,' that he really wanted me. But the director and producer had the final say, no matter how hard Will fought for me. Of course, they made the wrong choice. Will knew that. He knew everything."

Kasey felt sick, painfully aware that Will probably didn't even remember having seen the woman. Abby was insane, and she had no chance against her, no choice but to keep her talking.

To what avail? To stall—until Will got here. Kasey didn't know how much time had passed. What seemed like hours might have only been minutes. She didn't know how long she'd been unconscious—maybe just long enough for Abby to tie her up. Kasey tried unsuccessfully to read the hands on her watch and cursed herself for coming home before Will expected her.

"So you kept in touch with him?" Kasey asked wearily.

Abby smiled again. "Of course. I called him and tried to see him, but he refused. I knew why. It was a test to see if I really loved him. And I do."

"But you broke into his house, Abby. Why?"

Abby looked at her as if Kasey were the demented one. "I had to see where he lived, didn't I? I had to let him know that I'd been there. I was a powerful force in his life, and Will needed to know that. He needed to pay attention to me. To me!" she repeated hysterically as she leaned toward Kasey, her face menacing.

Kasey shrank back in the wheelchair, too frightened to even draw a breath.

Abby seemed to gain control of herself. "Then he vanished, and I couldn't find him for weeks. I had a feeling he'd come to the city. I'm very intuitive about Will. Finally, I found him."

"How?" Kasey asked, sure that she knew.

"I saw him on television in that silly T-shirt. He'd worn it before, at my audition. I knew as soon as I saw his image on TV that he wore the shirt as a sign for me to come for him." She leaned forward again, looking Kasey right in the eye. "Then I saw you, and I knew you were the interfering bitch who was keeping him from me!"

Abby laughed, but there was no joy in the sound. "It was time for me to play the best role of my life, and you fell for it. You fell for Mrs. Janek like a ton of bricks. That's why I knew you'd be here tonight. You were just too good-hearted to turn down a plea from your poor old neighbor." She cackled again. "Weren't you friendly, though, so eager to help? Even bringing me pastries. Oh, I knew you were keeping the chocolate one for Will. I knew that was his favorite. I've researched every aspect of his life." She leaned closer. "I know everything about him."

"You're a very good actress," Kasey managed to say. "You were very convincing in both roles."

"Damn right. You never caught on to the tricks at your stupid restaurant, did you? Oh, it was so much fun to see you running around in circles."

Subtly, Abby's face changed. "But now I'm tired of games, and I'm very tired of you. I want you gone. Out of my life, out of Will's life. Forever. We'll all be better off when that happens. Things are winding down now. We're ready for the final curtain. Do you know what that means, Kasey?"

Kasey licked her dry lips, now totally unable to speak. Where was Will? It must be midnight by now. Why wasn't he looking for her? Perspiration trickled down her forehead. Her head pounded. Her heart raced. She was helpless, tied to a wheelchair. This couldn't be happening to her, Kasey told herself, closing her eyes tightly. It was a bad dream. A nightmare. When she opened her eyes, it would be over, and Abby would be gone.

But Abby wasn't gone; in fact, she was only inches away, bending over the wheelchair. Her words made Kasey's blood run cold.

"You're going to die, Kasey. Oh, I had my chance at the subway stop but Will saved you. And the car... You were inches from death. Mere inches. But there's no escape now, bitch!" She lowered her voice dramatically. "The time has come."

WILL STRETCHED his arms above his head and smiled. He'd rewritten a tough scene tonight, one that had been giving him problems for weeks. His head was suddenly clear, his thoughts concise.

Will had to laugh at himself for his romantic mood. Suddenly, he felt like a different man—coming clean with Kasey had set him free. He was certain that things would work out.

The writing was going very well, and so was their relationship—despite worries about the stalker. If only the police could get the woman out of his life, he thought wryly, everything would be perfect. He'd heard nothing from them and decided to call first thing in the morning. He'd light a fire under the New York police department and at least make sure they were in contact with the cops in Connecticut. Not that they were any more interested in the case than the ones here, but at least they could corroborate Will's story about being stalked.

He glanced at his watch. Midnight. Kasey should be here anytime. He turned off the computer, got up and went into the kitchen. He'd done a little shopping early in the day so they could share a late supper. Eventually, he planned to show off his cooking talent, but tonight they'd have a meal courtesy of the deli and wine store—two varieties of cold pasta salad, a special California chardonnay and apple strudel.

He set the table, complete with a bouquet of paper white narcissus, which he'd caught a glimpse of at Windows. He knew Kasey liked them, and he finally managed to track them down after calling a dozen florists. He wanted the night to be as perfect as possible.

After a cool shower, Will put on khaki pants, a white polo shirt, and slipped his bare feet into a pair of topsiders. He felt optimistic despite the threat that still hung over them. It certainly wouldn't keep him from being with Kasey.

But where was she? He'd actually expected her to come home early tonight, at least by twelve, and it was twelve-twenty. Had she come in and gone to her place even though he'd told her not to? Probably. She was so damned stubborn. He reached for the phone and punched in her number.

It rang ten times before he hung up.

Maybe she was still at work. With all the emergencies piling up at Windows, he wouldn't be surprised. He pulled out the phone book and found the number. But all he got was the answering machine giving the restaurant's hours and location. Checking the phone book again, Will found Judy's number. Kasey had promised she'd share a taxi with her friend.

Judy answered on the second ring.

"Judy. This is Will Eastman." He didn't wait for her response. "Did you and Kasey share a taxi tonight? She's not home yet and—"

"Oh, my God."

Will's heart jumped at her exclamation.

"I let her out nearly an hour ago. I watched her go into the building. I waited until she waved. Tim was right there—"

Will hung up the phone and headed out the door. He hit the elevator button again and again. "Come on, come on," he muttered, aware that he was probably overreacting. More than likely, Kasey was talking to Tim or Mr. Lemnos. Or visiting with Glenna. There was bound to be a simple explanation.

The elevator finally appeared, and Will jumped onto it. If there *was* a simple explanation, why was he feeling so damned anxious? She wasn't that late. Not yet. He burst into the lobby the moment the doors slid open.

Expecting Tim, he was surprised to see an unfamiliar face at the doorman's stand.

"Where's Tim?" he asked almost rudely.

"He went off duty at midnight. I'm Curtis."

Without introducing himself, Will asked, "Do you know Kasey Halliday?"

"Sure do."

"Have you seen her tonight?"

Curtis shook his head. "Not since I came on. She probably came in during Tim's shift."

"She's not home yet."

"Well, sometimes Ms. Halliday works late. She—"

"No! Don't you understand? She got off about an hour ago, and the taxi let her out right in front. Tim saw her—"

"Well, like I said, Tim's off duty."

Will felt perspiration break out on his face as he turned away and almost leapt back on the elevator, pushing the button frantically.

When the car stopped at nineteen, he went to Kasey's door first, knocked loudly and called her name.

No answer.

He headed for Glenna's. She wasn't home, but the Kramers were. And Russ Kramer wasn't happy to be wakened after midnight.

"What the hell's going on with you people? First the police, and now this," the sleepy Kramer demanded.

"I'm looking for Kasey Halliday. I know she's in the building somewhere—"

"Well, she's not in this apartment, buddy. I haven't seen her in days. So would you please leave us alone and let us get some sleep for a change? This damned building is getting to me," he said as he shut the door in Will's face.

Will tried the door of the vacant apartment. Locked tight. Then he headed to 1901. Suddenly, he was sure that Kasey had gone to check on the old woman who lived beside her. That was the answer. As soon as he knocked, she'd open the door and laugh at him for his concern. It was going to be fine. Kasey was all right. In fact, he thought he heard her voice coming from the woman's apartment.

He knocked softly. No one answered. He knocked again, louder this time. The apartment was deathly quiet. His knocking became a pounding. "Kasey, are you in there? Come to the door! Mrs.—" Hell, he couldn't remember the old woman's name. "Kasey," he called again. "Answer me!"

Frustrated, he threw his weight against the door. It held firm. Feeling crazed, he continued to throw himself against it again and again, pounding with his fists, and yelling Kasey's name. He had a gut feeling she was inside that apartment. Not being able to get to her almost drove him out of his mind. She was there—he knew it! There was nowhere else for her to be. The stalker must have used the old woman to lure Kasey inside.

He had to get into the apartment!

THE POUNDING STOPPED, and Abby took her hand away from Kasey's mouth. "Don't say a word," she threatened.

Kasey nodded. Did Will know she was inside? What if he walked away and stopped looking for her? No! He wouldn't. But where was he now?

"I've changed my mind," Abby said, hurriedly pushing the wheelchair into the living room.

Kasey let out her breath in a long sigh, and then her relief turned to icy fear as Abby reached in her handbag and pulled out a gun. She was pointing it at Kasey's head. "We're all going to die."

Kasey gasped.

"We're going to die together."

For a moment, Kasey thought she was going to faint. Her own death flashed before her eyes. She saw it happening vividly, the gun going off in a flash of red-and-black powder, the bullet entering her brain.

Then she sat up straight, pulling herself together, and spoke to Abby, her words rumbling out in a croak. "You love him, Abby. You know that's all that matters to you—your love for Will."

Abby looked confused, her eyes wildly darting about. "But nothing is working out right!" she wailed. "You've ruined it. Will shouldn't care if you disappear. He should be glad! But he's searching for you. That's not what I planned."

Kasey's thoughts bounced around frantically until she found an answer. "Let him in, Abby. We'll talk to him. I'm sure if we explain everything, he'll understand how much you love him—"

For a moment, Abby hesitated. "Once I thought there might be a chance for us in spite of you, but now I know I was wrong. He loves you. So that means the end—for you and Will, for all of us."

Kasey gave a little moan. She was too terrified to speak.

Abby smiled, a frighteningly eerie wisp of a smile. "Yes," she said, her eyes lighting up crazily. "Yes! I'll kill you both. Then—then I'll kill myself! I can't have him now, but I'll have him in death. You'll see! He won't be yours—not ever. He'll be mine, mine!"

As if in a trance, Abby walked to the balcony doors, opened them and stepped outside. "If I know Will, he'll be coming for you across the balconies. He'll pause here at the doors and see you tied in the wheelchair. I'll raise my gun . . . and you'll watch him die."

Kasey's hands clenched and unclenched. Then her fingers touched the wheelchair controls and she remembered that the chair was motorized.

Abby continued to talk, wrapped up in her soliloquy. "It didn't have to end this way. Will would have been mine if you'd stayed out of his life. But oh, no, you had to turn him away from me . . . Now all our deaths are on your head."

Keeping her eyes focused on Abby, Kasey moved her fingers on the controls. She heard a slight hum and knew it was just a matter of choosing the right button. Taking a deep breath, she pushed down, and the chair lunged forward, straight toward Abby.

It took the woman a moment to react. A moment too long. The chair hit her full force, driving her back toward the edge of the balcony. The gun flew out of her hand. Pinned against the railing, Abby began to scream.

FROM THE EDGE of the balcony, Will froze, taking in the chilling scene before him—a woman trapped against the railing, Kasey tied to a lunging wheelchair, fumbling desperately with the controls.

Before he could move, the railing behind the woman broke with a loud crack, and her scream pierced the night air as she fell backward, hurtling down, down, to the pavement, nineteen stories below.

The wheelchair stopped, caught on the broken railing, but its wheels kept spinning, its motor grinding on.

"Be still, Kasey, don't move! You'll upset the balance—"

His warning came too late. One wheel lurched forward over the edge, and the chair tilted toward the terrible void. The motor churned on, and Kasey began to scream.

Will hit the balcony running, lunged to Kasey and grabbed the wheelchair from behind. But he couldn't move it, couldn't pull it back.

"Oh, God, I'm going to fall. I'm going to die!" Kasey cried.

"No, you aren't. I won't let you, but you have to be still. Freeze, Kasey." He moved away from her.

"Will—"

"Wait for me, and *don't even breathe*."

Will sprinted across the balcony and through the doors, heading for Kasey's kitchen. Wildly, he opened drawers, scattering cutlery on the floor, cursing the wasted time. Ten seconds, fifteen. His heart pounded frantically. How long would the railing hold?

He grabbed the first knife he touched and raced back to her. The wheelchair had begun to move, gradually but steadily. He could feel it shift. Perspiration poured down his face; his breath came in ragged gasps as he used the knife to saw the ropes that bound Kasey's arms.

Kasey sobbed and called his name. He had to save her. All he needed was a few more seconds!

Her hands were free! Holding her against his body, he leaned over into the empty space nineteen floors above the street, cut through the ropes around her ankles and swept Kasey into his arms. The chair, no longer balanced by her weight, plunged into the dark night.

Epilogue

WILL'S COTTAGE was set far back from the highway, down a tree-lined winding dirt road. It seemed to Kasey as if they were a million miles from New York City. Will had made no attempt to cut back the brush and brambles that twined around a split-rail fence. Oak and maple trees sheltered the wood-and-stone cottage that overlooked a rolling meadow, fragrant with summer flowers.

"Wild and untamed," Kasey murmured. "Just the way I like it."

"Talking about me?" Will joined her on the porch steps and gave her a lingering kiss.

"You *and* the house. It's perfect."

"A great place to write and concentrate, but it can get lonely."

"So can New York City." Putting her arms around his waist, she kissed him thoughtfully and gave his T-shirt a little tug. "You're wearing it again, I see."

Will looked down at his chartreuse shirt with the huge purple eye. "I decided it was time to take off the hex and wear it in the sunshine with the woman I love."

"I like the sound of that. 'The woman I love,'" she repeated softly before kissing him again, slowly, nibbling at his lips, tasting him, loving him. The more Kasey was with Will, the more she wanted him. Of all the amazing things that had happened to her during the past weeks, that was the most amazing—and the most wonderful.

She rested her head against his shoulder. "I still feel guilty that I dragged you to the park that day."

"You didn't make me wear this shirt, Kasey. Who knows why I picked it? I knew there was a risk going out in daylight no matter what I was wearing. Hell, sooner or later, Abby would have tracked me down, somehow."

"What a tangled web of events," Kasey mused aloud. "And it all began when the elevator at Bartow Tower stalled." She flashed him an impish grin. "If I'd listened to my friends, I never would have struck up a conversation with a stranger, and you and I would never have met—or fallen in love."

"Mmm." He moved his hand along her shoulder to her breast, eliciting a little gasp from Kasey. "Fallen *madly* in love," he corrected.

"You see, there is something good to be said about being friendly." She snuggled close to him.

"I have an idea we would have gotten together anyway. It was fate, Kasey. But your outgoing personality made it happen sooner. Thanks for that extra time." He kissed her again. "Even if we had to spend it in Bartow Horror."

"As far as I'm concerned, the only redeeming feature of that place is that it brought us together. Thank heavens my lease is up next month."

"Perfect timing."

Kasey was curious. "Why perfect?"

He lifted her hand to his lips and kissed her palm. "I was thinking, wondering . . . if you would want to—" He shook his head in amusement. "Listening to me now, no one would ever believe that I make my living with words."

"What is the famous television writer trying to say?"

"Just this. I'll be direct. Would you like to move in with me? Make things permanent?"

Kasey was quiet.

Will tightened his arm around her. "You're making me very nervous."

"I love you, Will Mastane." She laughed. "It's taking some getting used to—your real name. But Eastman or Mastane, I love you. But your cottage in the woods is—"

"A little too primitive for you?"

"No! I like the wild and wonderful feeling here. But it's a long commute to my job at Windows. I'm getting a handle on the job, and doing really well—"

"That you are. And what you're telling me is that you don't want to give it up. You don't want to leave the city," Will said flatly.

"Yes and no. Now that Fred's back, I'll have some time off, and I'd love to spend it here with you. In fact, I'd love to spend all my time off here."

"That's more like it," he said, planting a kiss on her forehead. "And what about the other time?"

"I was thinking you might want to spend some of it in the city."

"Now that I have a reason, you bet I would. A home in the country, a *pied à terre* in the city. Very chic.

Sounds like the perfect life. So where will our New York hideaway be? Another high rise?"

"No way," Kasey said emphatically. "Something on the ground floor."

"A romantic brownstone apartment, maybe?"

"Yes," she agreed. "With a nice sunny bedroom . . ."

"And a little private garden . . ."

"Where we'll live happily ever after." Kasey sighed and settled into his arms. The setting sun blazed across the meadow and bathed them both in its golden glow. She held on tightly to Will. Thinking about all the days and nights ahead of them, she laughed softly.

"What is it, darling?"

"I was just fantasizing."

"About me and you?" he asked.

"Yes."

"You don't have to fantasize anymore. I'm right here." He kissed her deeply.

She put her arms around him and felt his body, hard and strong beneath her hands. "Yes," she murmured. "You're very, very real. Sometimes fantasies do come true."

COMING NEXT MONTH

#557 PASSION AND SCANDAL Candace Schuler
Bachelor Arms Book 9

Welcome to Bachelor Arms, a trendy L.A. apartment building, where you'll bump into colorful neighbors and hear gossip about the tenants. Gossip such as: What *really* happened in apartment 1-G years ago? Willow Ryan puts Steve Hart's investigative skills—and his passionate feelings for her—to the test when she decides to uncover the scandalous truth.

#558 KISS OF THE BEAST Mallory Rush
Secret Fantasies Book 10

Do you have a secret fantasy? Researcher Eva Campbell does. She's an expert on virtual reality, and in her computer she's created the perfect man. Except, her fantasy lover is much more real than she could *ever* imagine....

#559 THE DRIFTER Vicki Lewis Thompson
Urban Cowboys Book 2

A Stetson and spurs don't make a man a cowboy. But New York truck driver, Chase Lavette, could have been born on a ranch. And like most cowboys, he was a drifter who avoided any form of commitment. But then gorgeous Amanda Drake came to the True Love ranch, bringing with her the son Chase never knew he had!

#560 MAKE-BELIEVE HONEYMOON Kristine Rolofson

Jilted and jobless...but that was no reason *not* to go on her honeymoon Kate Stewart decided. London, England, was the homeplace of many of her fantasies: dashing lords and flirtatious ladies. Besides, Kate was beginning to realize she wasn't all that heartbroken! Especially after she met the dark and brooding Duke of Thornecrest....

AVAILABLE NOW:

Take 4 bestselling love stories FREE

Plus get a FREE surprise gift!

Special Limited-time Offer

Mail to Harlequin Reader Service®

3010 Walden Avenue
P.O. Box 1867
Buffalo, N.Y. 14269-1867

YES! Please send me 4 free Harlequin Temptation® novels and my free surprise gift. Then send me 4 brand-new novels every month, which I will receive before they appear in bookstores. Bill me at the low price of $2.66 each plus 25¢ delivery and applicable sales tax, if any.* That's the complete price and a savings of over 10% off the cover prices—quite a bargain! I understand that accepting the books and gift places me under no obligation ever to buy any books. I can always return a shipment and cancel at any time. Even if I never buy another book from Harlequin, the 4 free books and the surprise gift are mine to keep forever.

142 BPA AWSV

Name	(PLEASE PRINT)	
Address		Apt. No.
City	State	Zip

This offer is limited to one order per household and not valid to present Harlequin Temptation® subscribers. *Terms and prices are subject to change without notice. Sales tax applicable in N.Y.

HARLEQUIN®

Temptation®

Secret Fantasies

Do you have a secret fantasy?

Researcher Eva Campbell does. She's an expert on
virtual reality and in her computer she's created the
perfect man. Except her fantasy lover is much more
real than she could ever imagine.... Experience
love with the ideal man in Mallory Rush's #558
KISS OF THE BEAST, available in October.

Everybody has a secret fantasy. And you'll find them
all in Temptation's exciting new yearlong miniseries,
Secret Fantasies. Throughout 1995 one book each
month focuses on the hero or heroine's innermost
romantic desires....

MOVE OVER, MELROSE PLACE!

> Apartment for rent
> One bedroom
> Bachelor Arms
> 555-1234

Come live and love in L.A. with the tenants of Bachelor Arms. Enjoy a year's worth of wonderful love stories and meet colorful neighbors you'll bump into again and again.

Startling events from Bachelor Arms' past return to stir up scandal, heartache and painful memories for three of its tenants. Read popular Candace Schuler's three sexy and exciting books to find out how passion, love and betrayal at Bachelor Arms affect the lives of three dynamic men. Bestselling author of over fifteen romance novels, Candace is sure to keep you hooked on Bachelor Arms with her steamy, sensual stories.

LOVERS AND STRANGERS #549 (August 1995)

SEDUCED AND BETRAYED #553 (September 1995)

PASSION AND SCANDAL #557 (October 1995)

Next to move into Bachelor Arms are the heroes and heroines in books by ever-popular Judith Arnold!

Don't miss the goings-on at Bachelor Arms

HARLEQUIN®
Temptation.

Become a
Privileged Woman,
You'll be entitled to all
these *Free Benefits.*
And *Free Gifts,* too.

To thank you for buying our books, we've designed an exclusive FREE program called *PAGES & PRIVILEGES™.* You can enroll with just one Proof of Purchase, and get the kind of luxuries that, until now, you could only read about.

Big HOTEL DISCOUNTS

A privileged woman stays in the finest hotels. And so can you—at up to 60% off! Imagine standing in a hotel check-in line and watching as the guest in front of you pays $150 for the same room that's only costing you $60. Your *Pages & Privileges* discounts are good at Sheraton, Marriott, Best Western, Hyatt and thousands of other fine hotels all over the U.S., Canada and Europe.

Free DISCOUNT TRAVEL SERVICE

A privileged woman is always jetting to romantic places.

When you fly, just make one phone call for the lowest published airfare at time of booking— or double the difference back!

PLUS—you'll get a $25 voucher to use the first time you book a flight AND 5% cash back on every ticket you buy thereafter through the travel service!